Task Force

John Simpson

Published by
Dreamspinner Press
4760 Preston Road
Suite 244-149
Frisco, TX 75034
http://www.dreamspinnerpress.com/

This is a work of fiction. Names, characters, places and incidents either are the product of the author's imagination or are used fictitiously, and any resemblance to actual persons, living or dead, business establishments, events or locales is entirely coincidental.

Task Force
Copyright © 2008 by John Simpson

Cover Art by Dan Skinner/Cerberus Inc. cerberusinc@hotmail.com
Cover Design by Mara McKennen

All rights reserved. No part of this book may be reproduced or transmitted in any form or by any means, electronic or mechanical, including photocopying, recording, or by any information storage and retrieval system without the written permission of the Publisher, except where permitted by law. To request permission and all other inquiries, contact Dreamspinner Press, 4760 Preston Road, Suite 244-149, Frisco, TX 75034
http://www.dreamspinnerpress.com/

ISBN: 978-1-935192-15-2

Printed in the United States of America
First Edition
September, 2008

eBook edition available
eBook ISBN: 978-1-935192-16-9

This book is dedicated to Sarah and Jimison Hutchinson who have become good friends and are responsible for my dynamic new website. Sarah is a talented web creator who gave her talents to improve my public persona. Jimison, ever wordy, contributed to the copy edit along with his humor *inscrutabilis*. May our lives be ever-connected.

Chapter One
Time Heals All Wounds

IT had been two weeks since the Christian fundamentalist Milford clan had ended their existence on this Earth by blowing themselves up rather than face arrest, ending their rampage of antigay murders. They didn't like it when they were finally cornered by the police for conducting their own personal "holy war" against the gay community of Prince George County, Maryland. Officer Patrick St. James had been on light duty since the event, at the suggestion of the department shrink. Patrick had experienced extensive violence over a relatively short period of time, including having taken a human life in the line of duty. This act, perhaps more than almost anything else that a police officer experiences, is the most stressful.

After the incident, Dean, Patrick's wonderful new lover, had spent every free minute with him. They had become inseparable. Patrick felt great comfort with Dean and believed that he was truly lucky to have found him. When they made love he forgot about time and space; the only thing that mattered in the universe was this wonderful man, this incredible lover. Dean remained uncomfortable with Patrick being a police officer, especially after the Milford case. They had the same talk that every couple, straight or gay, has when one partner is a cop. Dean wanted to make sure Patrick came home at the end of each shift, unhurt and whole, in every sense of the word.

Pat hurried home, as it was his last day shift for some time to come. He was hoping to surprise Dean by having supper ready for him when he got home. As Pat pulled into the driveway, he looked in the rearview mirror and saw that Dean was right behind him.

Getting out of their cars, they smiled at each other.

"Damn. I was going to have dinner waiting for you when you got home, but you just took care of that."

"Well, I remembered this was your last day shift for some time to come and I wanted to be home early. You want to go out for dinner instead of slaving over a hot stove?"

"Sure, but let me take a shower first," Pat said with a smile that communicated its own message.

Dean laughed and they entered the coolness of the house.

Pat took off his uniform, hung his police gear in the downstairs closet and went upstairs to the bedroom, throwing a look over his shoulder to see if Dean was watching. He stripped down to nothing and walked to the bathroom to get in the shower, where he found Dean naked and sitting on the tub. Dean had made a mad dash to the bathroom while Pat was disrobing in order to surprise him. He looked down at Pat's now growing dick and licked his lips.

"Well, this is a nice surprise. You plan on doing something with those lips besides lick 'em?" Pat asked with an obvious leer.

Dean reached over and turned the water on, got the temperature right, and motioned for his lover to get in with him. As the warm water cascaded off Pat's back and down the crack of his ass, Pat felt Dean's lips slowly kiss each ass cheek. Pat loved it when Dean did this, and Dean knew it. Once Pat grew completely hard, he turned around and saw Dean, who was now on his knees with the water splashing off his face. Dean's dick was also rigid and begging for attention. As Pat looked down at Dean's beautiful manhood, Dean took his lover's dick into his mouth and started to gently suck. He reached up with his right hand and fondled Pat's balls as he sucked the full length of his shaft. As Pat began to moan softly, Dean reached around with his left hand and began to caress Pat's right ass cheek. Pat was now fully consumed by the feelings that were coursing through his body. He wished those feelings would never stop.

Pat pulled out of Dean's hungry mouth as he felt himself begin to build toward a climax; it was way too early for that. Pat reached down and grabbed Dean's hands and pulled him to his feet. He kissed Dean deeply and with all the passion he felt for him. As Pat continued to kiss Dean, he began to think that this might be the man he would be very happy to spend the rest of his life with. He had fantastic looks, great brains, and a bright future. And he was fantastic in bed. What more could Pat wish for?

Pat broke from the kiss and slid down to his own knees, landing directly in front of Dean's engorged cock. The perfect beauty of his penis always stunned Pat, and he drove his mouth onto it with all the lust that was within him. Pat heard Dean let out a whimper as he began to vigorously suck him. He cupped Dean's balls in his hand and realized that he had shaved them; they were smooth and large to the touch. Pat took great pride in being able to take Dean's entire dick down his throat, which gave him vast pleasure. He began to moan loudly now as Pat sucked harder and harder, increasing the speed of his motion on his partner's cock. When he felt Dean's hands tighten on his head and saw his balls start to climb up under his cock, Pat stopped his sucking action.

"No, you don't! I have something else in mind for you, mister," Pat said with a smile. He stood up and told Dean, "Turn around, stud."

As Dean turned around Pat looked down and saw the magnificent mounds of his ass and almost blew his load right then and there. He grabbed both cheeks with his hands and kneaded them and caressed them, reaching around at one point to grab his lover's dick and stroke it a few times. Pat kissed and nibbled on Dean's neck and reached for the soap. He lathered up his cock and pushed some soap into Dean's butt hole, and then pressed his dick into the man he loved. Dean bent over in the tub and Pat slowly entered him, inch by inch. Dean moaned and urged him on, so Pat pushed all the way in and let it rest once inside.

Pat's mind exploded with a kaleidoscope of colors as he felt the searing heat of Dean's ass envelope his cock. He started to slowly move in and out of Dean, enjoying every bit of movement. Between the feeling of the water lashing over their bodies and the pure joy of ass-fucking Dean, he began to cum much sooner than he would have liked.

"Ahh, shit, I'm cumming," he moaned with disappointment.

"That's okay, babe. Give it to me, pound my ass!"

With that he emptied himself into Dean and felt intense relief wash over his body. As Dean straightened up in the shower, he turned around and kissed Pat even deeper than before.

"How would you like to get off my dear, hips or lips?" Pat asked with a laugh.

"I already did get off. I came while you were fucking me," came the response to Pat's question accompanied by a big smile.

"Nice, babe. Let's finish showering and get out of here before we turn into prunes."

As they finished drying off in the bedroom, Dean looked at Pat and said, "Ya know, I really care for you a lot and I don't want anything to happen to you. Would you ever consider giving up being a cop and come to work at the bank in the security department?"

"No, Dean, that's just not me. I enjoy being a cop and it's all I ever wanted to do. I know it's dangerous, but that's part of the allure for me. I like the danger."

"But if you worked at the bank, we wouldn't have to be as careful about being gay and our being lovers."

"Maybe so, but I just wouldn't be as happy in my work. Don't you understand that being a cop is more than just what I do for work, it's who and what I am?"

"Okay, I understand, I guess. Suddenly I don't feel like going out for dinner. Why don't we order some Chinese for delivery?"

"Okay; you know what I like. I'll see if there is anything worth watching on HBO. I think 'Deadwood' is on tonight."

Chapter Two
Return to Action

THE next evening it was time for Pat to get ready for work. He was returning to the midnight shift, which is where he liked to be. Dean and Pat had finished dinner, and Pat got up and began to get prepared for work. Pat noticed that he was being watched by his lover with a kind of nervous energy that was uncomfortable.

"Dean, you just have to relax about my job. I'm gonna be fine. I am well-trained, working with a bunch of other cops who are well-trained, and I like it. You need to relax or you'll become a ball of nerves every night and we just can't have that."

"Yeah, you're right, but I can't help the way I feel. I'll work on it, that I promise," he said with a smile.

Pat was more concerned about returning to his buddies and the active police environment than being hurt. He needed to make sure they didn't find out he was gay. He still worked with a lot of guys who just didn't like gay people, and they didn't seem like they would ever be changing their minds. At least he no longer had to ride with Flanders. Because of the major case Pat had just finished, he was being cut loose to ride by himself. He would have his own beat car and be responsible for a particular area of the county. Pat looked at his watch and saw that it was almost 9:30 p.m. He was due at roll call in thirty minutes. He quickly finished dressing, kissed Dean, flew out of the house, and left for the station.

As he walked into the roll call room, he noticed almost everyone had arrived before him. Sergeant Durkin looked up and nodded at him. "Welcome back, St. James. Good to have you with us."

"Thanks, Sarge," he replied, as the others all greeted him.

He settled into his seat and started to read the BOLO reports that told everyone what to look for during their shifts. Stolen cars were always the number-one item on the listing. From the look of things, it appeared to have been pretty quiet since the explosion and death of the right-wing clan from the Midwest.

"Roll call!" yelled Durkin to get the room quiet.

"All right, gentlemen, as you can see we have our star rookie back with us tonight. St. James resumes normal patrol duties, so we are back to full strength in the squad."

The Sergeant went down the list, assigning each man a beat car, and Pat finally heard his name and assignment.

"St. James, you have Adam 5 tonight. You did such a good job in that sector before, we'll just see if you can keep it up. Flanders, that moves you to Adam 9, and Capstone, you'll ride alone in Adam 6 and back up Adam 5 on calls. Any questions? Then hit the streets!"

Roll call was over and everyone got up to head to the armory to check out shotguns and then slide into the night in their cruisers. Hank and Pat had exchanged a few words and agreed to meet later for coffee at one of the numerous 7 Elevens that dotted the county like fleas on a dog.

"Don't get shot, St. James! I'm not there to babysit you anymore!" shouted Flanders.

"You worry about yourself there, Corporal. That should keep you busy enough to stay out of trouble!" he yelled back, as he pulled out of the station parking lot and headed toward his beat in College Park. College Park: playground for all the boys and girls from the University of Maryland, which was just down the street. If it weren't for the university, College Park wouldn't exist.

Since the first couple of hours were quiet, Pat decided to meet up with Hank. He switched to the private frequency that went inter-car only, and called for him.

"Adam 5, Adam 6?"

"Adam 6. Go ahead, Pat."

"You wanna eighty-two at the 7-Eleven on Central Avenue and Forty-Sixth Street?"

"Ten-four, en route."

It would take them both just a couple of minutes to meet at the 7-Eleven and get the coffee that would help them stay awake all night if there were no calls. He felt hungry as well and he knew he would end up getting a cop's favorite food: the doughnut. What a joy and a relief to have another gay officer on the squad who had become a close friend. Thanks once again to part gaydar, and part rumor, Hank and Pat had had one of those awkward chats where you try to find out if a guy is gay or not. A hooker at a squad pool party did the rest to make it obvious to Hank that Pat was gay. The real luck was in their being assigned together because of their ages and looks, to catch the killers who were targeting gay men in the Milford case. The department thought it was heroic of them to work undercover in gay bars posing as gay men. Little did they know.

Now they were practically partners as they worked adjoining beat cars.

Pat pulled in first just as Hank was turning the corner to come into the parking lot. They got out, went into the store, and got some coffee and a doughnut, like he knew he would. As they sat in their cruisers sipping the coffee, conversation flowed easily. He had come to like Hank a lot after working so closely with him on the serial murder case.

"So, how's the love life, Pat? Is Dean treating you right?"

"Ah, couldn't be better," he answered with a smile. "Dean is like a dream come true. He really is a remarkable man. He isn't just good looks; he has a big heart and really cares about people. What about you? Seeing anyone?"

"Nothing serious. Just a couple of one-night stands."

"Well, maybe we can all go out on a double date kinda thing one of these days. I think that would be fun."

"Adam 5, Adam 6, handle priority a 13F at the Schoolhouse Bar and Grill, Nine Six Four University Boulevard. Complainant is the bar manager, who states that seven to ten males are engaged in a fight on the main dance floor area. No weapons seen."

"Adam 5 and Adam 6 en route."

"Well, time to go to work, Hank!" Pat said, as they sped off to the fight call with lights and sirens.

As they sliced through the night en route to the bar, they heard Adam 4 and Adam 7 tell dispatch that they too were responding. *Good,* Pat thought. *That's four of us at least, which should be enough.* Traffic was light, as it was almost two in the morning and most good people were home in bed. As they entered the block on which the bar was located, they saw college kids pouring out of the bar, some of whom were covered in beer. It had obviously gotten wild during the fight. "Adam 5 and 6 out at the 13F."

"Ten-four, Adam 5 and 6, 0157 hours."

As Hank and Pat entered the bar, the smell of beer was overwhelming. They heard the fight coming from the back so that's where they headed. A bouncer with a bloody nose ran up to them and yelled, "It's way out of control. Those guys are drunk off their asses and aren't feeling any pain. I hit a couple of them hard and got nowhere!"

"Adam 5, keep 'em coming," Pat yelled into the mic. This told the other units that were responding that they were needed, along with anyone else in the area. As they rounded the corner and entered the dance floor area, they saw at least nine kids throwing punches and falling all over the floor. Most of the guys were bloodied like the bouncer and gave no signs of letting up. Hank started to brush past Pat to get into the fracas, and Pat grabbed him and yelled, "Let's wait for backup! No sense in getting our asses kicked and looking like rookies."

He believed that in these kinds of situations it was better to let the antagonists wear themselves out on each other and then move in to arrest what was left. A minute later, the other officers that responded to the call entered the bar and joined them. Adam 10, the Sergeant, also responded, and was on-scene now.

"Okay, St. James and Capstone, you guys take the ones on the left, Delaney and Morris with me on the right. Let's go!"

With that they moved in on the drunken brawlers and started to pull them apart using their PR-24 nightsticks as needed. When they had one down, the drunk was cuffed and left on the floor; then they went after the next one. In no more than two minutes, all were under arrest and handcuffed. All the officers heard now was moaning and groaning from minor fight injuries and the almost constant whine that the cuffs were too tight. As the officers hauled them to their feet for transport down to the station, Durkin told Pat to get the information for the report from the manager and then head to the station to type it up. The other officers would process the prisoners and take them before the court for bail hearings.

P<small>AT</small> spent the rest of the shift typing up reports and finished just as the shift ended. It felt good to leave the stationhouse, get in his cruiser, and head for home. Now that Pat was no longer a trainee riding with Corporal Flanders, he got what was called a "take-home cruiser," which meant that his duty car went home with him. He was permitted to drive it while he was off-duty as well, as long as he didn't leave the county. It was part of a program to put more cruisers on the road, which made it appear as if more cops were working. Pat certainly didn't object; it saved him money on gas and wear and tear on his personal car.

Just as he arrived at home, Dean was getting up for the start of his workday.

"Good morning, sweetheart." Pat gave Dean a kiss on the lips.

"Good morning. How was work?"

"Not too exciting. Just a bunch of drunk, horny, good-looking frat boys, feeling their oats," he said with a smile, as he walked up the stairs to go to bed.

Chapter Three
Déjà Vu All Over Again

NOTHING much happened the rest of the week and, before Pat knew it, it was his weekend. In this rotation, he had Tuesday and Wednesday off. Trouble was that it was not the weekend for Dean. Like most of the world, his days off were Saturdays and Sundays. The only cops that got weekends off were desk jockeys and the brass. As a result, Pat had little to do when he got up in the late afternoon besides go to the gym, work out and take a swim.

He tried to keep his body in top shape; the job required it if he was to avoid getting many injuries. Besides, he never minded checking out the other guys at the gym, even though he was kinda married. No harm in looking and enjoying.

As he entered the steam room at the club, he noted only one other guy in there. He nodded to him as he sat down, keeping the towel wrapped around his waist. While the temperature was hot, it wasn't the kind of heat that made it hard to breathe. As Pat looked up, he saw that the other guy had opened his towel and was making sure Pat got a good look at what God gave him. He looked away after checking out his equipment and tried to remember that he had a boyfriend now and that he was a cop in this county.

As he looked back after a minute, the other guy was now jacking off lightly and smiling at him. Pat couldn't help but look down and admire his stuff.

"You wanna join me over here, guy?"

"No thanks, I gotta go anyway. Be careful. I hear there are cops that work out here," he said with a smile as he got up and walked away, proud of himself for turning down the hot stud with the hard-on.

"Not to worry. I can spot a cop a mile away."

As he entered the shower, he was grateful for the cold water pouring down on his body and taking some of the heat out of it. Normally, he wouldn't have done anything with the guy in the steam room, but he would have gotten his number or agreed to meet outside to go somewhere. He wasn't tempted to do either because he was so thankful to have Dean; a piece of ass wasn't worth jeopardizing that happiness. Maybe he was starting to grow up a little. The whole world wasn't just one big giant dick!

When he got home he saw that it was almost time for Dean to arrive. He quickly threw a premade dish into the oven, and went upstairs. He entered the bedroom and tore off his clothes and jumped onto the bed. He may not have tricked with that guy, but he sure was hot over the incident. Dean would greatly profit from this state of mind and body.

He heard the key go into the door lock and smiled.

"Hello, I'm home!"

"Hi. I'm up here just waking up."

Dean walked into the bedroom and saw him lying on the bed, naked, with a huge hard-on. He looked down, smiled, and asked, "Is that for me?"

"Well, it ain't for the milkman!"

Dean laughed out loud and started to slowly take off his clothes. When he was all the way down to his Calvin's, he said, "I'd better take a very quick shower first, stud. Don't want you hesitant to put your tongue anywhere you desire, now do I?"

With that he left the room quickly and got into the shower. The thought crossed Pat's mind to join him again, but he resisted, realizing that it would be more comfortable in bed. As he waited for Dean's return, he kept his rock-hard erection by thinking about the stud at the gym. He chastised himself for even thinking about that guy as he was about to make love to Dean.

Dean came back into the bedroom not fully dried off and lunged onto the bed. They kissed deeply and with great zeal. Pat pushed him down onto his back and lowered his lips to his partner's nipples where he began to gently lick each one, teasing it, making it hard. Dean began to moan with pleasure, as this was his main erogenous zone. Pat then worked his way down Dean's chest and stomach toward his now erect cock, which was waiting for Pat's full attention.

As he ran his tongue over Dean's shaft, Dean almost vibrated off the bed.

"Gawd, that's good!" he yelled.

With that kind of encouragement, Pat was motivated to make sure this was the best blowjob Dean had ever had. As he deep-throated him for what seemed like ten minutes, Dean continued to pull on Pat's hands to get him up to his face. He finally let go of Dean's cock when Dean tapped him on the head, which was the signal for, "Hello, I'm gonna cum if ya don't stop sucking."

Before Pat could kiss him again, he found himself on his stomach, not his back as he had anticipated. He thought he was in for a good fucking but instead of a probing finger he felt the warm, wet sensation of his lover's tongue on his ass. Pat virtually saw sparks when Dean drove his tongue deep into his asshole. His toes curled and he grabbed the headboard in pure ecstasy. If there was one thing that Dean excelled at in bed, it was eating ass!

Dean continued to drive Pat wild with this incredible pleasure until he begged for him to fuck him. He wanted nothing else at that point but to have Dean's cock driven repeatedly into his ass.

When he stopped, he reached over into the nightstand and retrieved the lube and rubbers.

"Don't you want some head first, Pat?"

"Fuck no, just shove your cock up my ass, Dean. I need to be fucked good!"

He felt the pressure against his opening from the head of Dean's cock and relaxed himself so that Dean could slowly enter him. As his cock sank deeper and deeper into his ass, Pat felt the primordial urge to become one with him.

"Fuck me, and fuck me hard!" he ordered. Dean's rim job had driven him over the edge of lust and he needed to get pounded.

"Okay, babe, you asked for it!"

With that Dean started to fuck his ass with increasing speed and deeper thrusts. It felt incredibly good to have his man fucking the hell out of his compliant ass. Dean reached down and pulled him up at the hips so that they were now fucking doggy style. This was Pat's favorite position and Dean knew it.

Pat started to stroke his cock as his ass was being well-fucked. He could feel Dean's balls slapping against his ass cheeks each time he drilled his cock into him. The faster he fucked, the faster he stroked his cock. Finally, he heard Dean start to moan, and he yelled, "Don't stop now; just finish it!"

With that Dean exploded into his ass, his body shaking violently. It was all Pat needed to climax and shoot all over the bed sheets. As his strokes slowed to a crawl, Dean finally collapsed onto Pat's back and they fell onto the bed. Dean could feel his cock start to slowly withdraw from deep within his lover's ass and he felt total contentment. He slipped out and rolled off onto his back.

"Incredible, Dean. I needed that." Pat smiled. "I don't know what got into you, but that was fantastic!"

He reached over and pulled the rubber off of Dean's cock and threw it into the trash can, then got up and went into the bathroom and leaped into the shower and rinsed the cum off of his body. He returned with a wet washcloth and wiped off Dean's cock and balls.

"Honey, let me change the sheets and then you just take a nap, and I'll call you for dinner," he gently said to Dean.

With that, he threw on his shorts and went down to the kitchen to make sure dinner was nearly ready.

TWO nights later, he was back on the Adam 5 beat once again. The ever-present summer humidity had been cut by a recent thunderstorm that had blown through the area. It was just after midnight when the call came out. A high-pitched tone signaled that an urgent emergency call was coming, and was followed by the call from dispatch:

"Adam 5, Adam 6, Mary 9, see the manager at the Fox Ridge Inn and Bar, Queens Chapel Road and Barrett Road. Report of a homicide at that location. Adam 5, handle priority."

"Adam 5, ten-four."

The "Fox Ridge Inn and Bar" was the new name of the motel-bar complex that used to be known as the "Jump It" bar and motel. The owners had changed the name after the murders of gay men by members of the right-wing religious group. In light of this call, it might have been a useless gesture. He couldn't help but think that they might not have gotten all of the killers from that group. Did one survive? *Please, God, no!*

Pat arrived on-scene and found the manager waiting outside. It was the same manager he'd dealt with during the Milford Clan investigations.

"Officer, I can't believe it. Not again!" the manager said.

"Okay, calm down. What did you find?" Pat asked, as he heard the approach of the other units.

"It's been a real quiet night and I was just about to light up a cigarette outside, when I got a call from the maintenance guy. He saw a door open and saw the dark outline of a guy on the floor in the dark."

"And?" Pat asked rather impatiently.

"After he found him he called me at the front desk and I ran to room five twenty-nine. I found the door open and the light off. I knocked and announced who I was and got no response. So, I entered the room and turned the light on and that's when I found the gentleman who appears to be dead."

"And did your maintenance guy see anyone leaving the room?"

"When I talked to him he said no. And by the time I got to room five twenty-nine, which is on the other side of the top balcony, someone could have left the room and I wouldn't have seen them."

"What do you have, St. James?" asked the homicide detective who had arrived on-scene.

"I don't know much yet—just got here—but we have a body in room five twenty-nine with no one seen leaving the crime scene. This is Mr. Morison, the night manager who called it in. He got a call from maintenance and when he got to the room he found our dead body."

Detectives Sheffield and Capstone and Pat headed up to the room, which had been locked up by the manager when the body was found. As they entered the room and turned on the light, they could smell the faint scent of death that occurs just after a person dies. The body was that of a white male, approximately twenty-four years old, black hair, blue eyes, about 6′2″ and 195 pounds. He was naked and his eyes were wide open, a look of surprise on his face. The room was fairly neat, except for the sheets and pillows, which had been moved about. It appeared that the deceased might have had sex before his death.

They took a closer look at the body and could see no obvious signs of trauma to the once good-looking, now deceased male. They found no evidence of another person having been in the room at all. It was possible that the death was by natural means.

"St. James, call the coroner and seal off the area for the evidence technicians. I want the entire room processed for prints and body fluids," Sheffield said. "Right now, we don't even know if we have a homicide here."

The coroner responded to the scene and removed the body after deciding he would need to do an autopsy to determine cause of death. Dr. Richards rarely gave guesses as to the cause of death at the scene unless there was an obvious sign, such as a gunshot wound to the head.

Pat was relegated to writing the report on the call and ended it with "pending investigation."

The rest of the shift went by without further incident.

A week later as Pat was getting dressed for work, Dean asked him a question. "How would you like to take one of those all-gay cruises we keep hearing about all the time? Danny and Mike went on one and said they had a blast. You can be yourself, and if I feel like kissing you during dinner in front of eighteen hundred guys, I can do it!"

Pat had to admit that the idea had some appeal to him. An entire enclosed environment where gay men and women could be themselves and taste the freedom that could be sounded great.

"Yeah, I think that would be kinda cool. Do you know what they cost?"

"Well, if we go to the Caribbean, there is an outfit called 'Ecstasy' that has prices from nine hundred dollars to about two thousand dollars. Really not bad, considering all the extras they throw in."

"I want a balcony cabin if we go. I'm more than fine with it! Make the arrangements and give me the dates so I can put in for vacation."

PAT went to work and, after taking a seat at roll call, he saw Homicide enter the squad room. Sergeant Durkin then introduced Detective Sheffield to the squad.

"Okay, listen up. Homicide is going to brief us on that body found last week at the gay motel."

"Gentlemen, we thought at first that we had a natural death on our hands, but as it turns out, the coroner has ruled the death a homicide.

The autopsy revealed two things. The cause of death was strangulation. This tidy little ending for the victim was assisted by a generous injection of morphine; in fact, three times the usual amount of morphine used to treat severe pain was found in the blood of the victim. It seems he was injected, and then when he was unable to resist, he was killed. There was postmortem bruising on his neck and the coroner's office isn't really sure what was used to strangle him.

"There were also signs that the victim had anal intercourse just before his death. There was no semen found, so we assume that a condom was used or the killer is shooting blanks."

"Do we have an ID on the victim?" Capstone asked.

"The victim is twenty-four-year-old Russell Moran, a rather well-known male prostitute who had a previous bust for soliciting an undercover Vice officer. He was convicted and sentenced to one-year probation, and has not been in trouble since then. Since we don't have any witnesses and very little to go on, you all need to keep your ears open for any rumors going around as to who killed our victim. Oh, one final thing: Forensics did pick up a blonde hair at the scene. Now this could be from the suspect, or from a previous guest in that room. We just don't know. Any questions?"

No one had any questions, so the squad was given their shift assignments and they broke for the road. Hank Capstone was driving the Adam 6 beat, so Pat and he would be working together as mutual backup on any calls that came out. The Sergeant had hinted that these would be permanent beat assignments, at least for a couple of months. As they were leaving to get into their patrol cars, the Sergeant smiled at Pat, for no apparent reason. It wasn't an evil smile, just a plain ol' smile. *Weird,* he thought.

Chapter Four
Street Life

As they all settled into their permanent beats each shift, the officers began to know the people who lived in their areas, and who belonged where and when. Hank and Pat had a great working relationship. Hank was turning into a good cop and a good friend, both of which were very good for Pat. The isolation that most gay cops felt was not an issue he had to deal with at this department.

It was a boring shift with almost no calls, so Pat parked and started to read the newspaper at a local restaurant that had been getting drunk patrons late at night. Sometimes just sitting in the parking lot was enough to stem the tide of disorderly clientele at some late-night businesses.

The only thing of interest in the *Annapolis Ledger,* which was the state political newsletter, was the fact that the governor, Dr. Keith Hanes, was pushing for a euthanasia law that would permit doctors to assist patients to exit life at a time of their own choosing. The Christian right was upset over this, and soundly condemned the Republican governor for even proposing such a thing.

"Adam 5 and Adam 6, report of a domestic dispute involving two brothers at two forty-eight East Main. Complainant is the neighbor at two fifty East Main, says she can hear yelling and fighting."

"Adam 5, ten-four."

"Adam 6, ten-four en route."

Pat and Hank arrived at the scene just a couple minutes later and went up to the door. They could hear yelling coming from inside. It sounded like a battle between domestic partners, not two brothers.

"Police!" they yelled, as they knocked on the door loudly.

It went quiet inside as the door slowly opened.

"We had a complaint that you two were fighting and disturbing the neighbors. What's going on?" Pat asked.

"Can we come in?" Hank asked.

The door swung fully open and they entered into what appeared to be a usually well-kept house, which was now in a state of chaos with pillows thrown everywhere and the coffee table overturned. Standing before them were two guys in their late twenties who were very good-looking and in shape. They both had red eyes from crying. One man was dressed only in underwear while the other was fully dressed. There were no signs of anyone being hit or injured.

"So, who wants to tell me what's going on?" Pat asked.

"Nothing we care to discuss," said the fully dressed guy.

"We understand you two are brothers. Is that true?"

"Well, not exactly," answered the guy in Calvin Klein's finest.

"So who are you, and what's going on?" he asked.

"My name is Joel, and this moron is Richard. No, we are not brothers; we are supposed to be lovers, or whatever you want to call it."

"Fuck you, Joel!"

"Okay, let's not get started again. What happened?" Hank asked.

"I came home from work and found this mess in bed with another man. His legs were so high in the air they left footprints on the ceiling!" Joel said.

Hank laughed out loud, and then apologized. Pat maintained his composure at the comment and asked what they planned to do for the rest of the night, as they did not want to be called back again.

"He's leaving and I don't care where he goes," said Joel.

"Fine, but you should know that your friend seduced me!"

Ouch! Not only did Joel's lover cheat on him, but he did it with a friend of Joel's. Both officers could see why things got heated.

"I don't care who seduced who; just get out!" yelled Joel.

"Okay, we're going to stand by here until Richard departs, and then we will leave. Who owns or rents this house?" Pat asked.

"We both rent this place," Joel answered.

"If both of your names are on the lease, than we can't force Richard to leave if he comes back tonight. You are going to have to decide whether or not this incident is enough to break you guys up, or give it another chance. But either way, he has as much right to live here as you do."

"For now, all I want is for his bony ass to be gone from here."

Richard muttered a goodnight to Joel before slamming the door on his way out of the house. Hank suggested that they might want to get counseling if they wanted to save their relationship. Joel looked at both officers in a funny manner when Hank offered this, as if it was the last thing he expected a cop to suggest to him.

"Good night, officers, and I'm sorry for you guys getting called out here."

"No problem. Just make sure we don't get called back," Hank said.

Chapter Five
Coffee and Lust

PAT was tired and a little worn down, as he was on the last day of his normal five-days-on- and-two-days-off rotation. Since there had been little excitement during the previous shifts this work week, he was hoping for some excitement tonight. Police work wasn't all right-wing clans blowing up gay bars and prostitute murders. On a normal shift he would have to deal with the mundane barking dog, landlord-tenant disputes and parking complaints, which begin to wear on every cop's nerves after a while.

As he patrolled his beat, he came upon one of the more interesting landlord-tenant disputes he'd seen since becoming a cop. A landlord had thrown all of the tenant's furniture out on the street and changed the locks while the tenant was at work, and both Pat and Hank had a hard time not smiling when they found out why. The landlord had walked in on the tenant and one of the landlord's family members in bed mid-stroke. It wasn't until the landlord started to relay all of the facts of the incident that they realized what was going on.

"I want him gone, right now! I found him fucking my son after he talked him into his bed. He seduced my innocent twenty-five-year-old son who is straight and has a girlfriend! They're even waiting to get married before having sex! This is how pure my Keith is!"

It was amazing how little the public realized about how much gay sex goes on. Up until the moment the landlord walked into that room, he thought his son was straight, and a top. Little did he know that his son was straight all right, straight for the next dick!

Pat stopped at the local 7-Eleven for his customary nightly cup of coffee; Capstone did what was quickly becoming the norm and met him there. Pat got out of his cruiser and stretched his legs as Capstone pulled into the parking lot and did the same. They entered the store and waved at the clerk, a twenty-two-year-old college student who had the build of a soccer player, and wore a name tag that said "Shawn." Capstone's eyes locked onto Shawn as they did every night; but he didn't want to cross any boundaries on duty and never said more than hello.

Pat headed back toward the coffee station in the rear of the store and asked the clerk if it had been a busy night.

"Nah, just a couple of freeloaders—I mean *cops*—stopping by," Shawn responded.

"Ha! Rather be a freeloader cop than a soda jerk in a 7-Eleven all my life," Pat responded as he chuckled, knowing that they went through this same routine humor every night as they cut on each other and then went about their business. He loved watching the twinkle in Shawn's eyes as they joked.

He could never quite figure out if Shawn was gay or not; sure, Shawn took care of himself, wore nice clothes and was extremely friendly whenever Capstone and Pat stopped in, but there wasn't a flamboyant bone in that boy's 5'11", one hundred and sixty pound body. Shawn had short spiked black hair, crystal blue eyes and a smile that would melt the polar ice caps. Pat thought to himself that he better be a good boy; Dean was at home waiting for him. Capstone had told him, however, that he always swore he saw something in the clerk's eyes that said, "I'm gay and I'm interested."

The coffee tasted like it had been on the burner for at least three hours. "Mmmm, the coffee's as fresh as ever. Do you ever bother to make fresh coffee?"

"Well, you get what you pay for," responded the cute college jock with his very sexy smile.

With that Pat walked out, clutching his free coffee. The local all-night stores always gave the cops free coffee to be assured they would come around more often. Sure, the coffee was lousy, but the price was right, and it had kept many of the boys in blue wide awake during the slowest of nights. 'Course, for this 7-Eleven clerk, Adam 5 and Adam 6 would have stopped in anyway! As for the stores, it was cheap insurance against robbery, as the cops came in and out repeatedly during the night.

Pat watched as Capstone made eye contact one last time with the clerk and walked out to join him, forgetting his coffee on the countertop. Just as Capstone realized what he had done, Shawn came running out with the coffee and a doughnut in a napkin. The clerk smiled at Capstone and said, "Hey, you forgot something. I threw in a doughnut for you because I thought you might get hungry during the night."

Pat laughed as Capstone blushed and muttered, "Oh, my coffee, thanks." As he began to turn away, Shawn said, "Well, yeah, your coffee too," and handed Capstone a neatly folded napkin before jogging back into the store. Pat watched as Capstone put his coffee and newly acquired doughnut on the hood of the cruiser and opened the napkin to find, neatly printed, "Shawn 555-0909."

After Capstone recovered from his shock, he looked into the giant plate-glass window and smiled. In response, Shawn gave a wink and then continued reading the previous day's newspaper.

Pat got into his cruiser, rolled down his window and told Capstone that he would see him later. Capstone, still dumbfounded at the whole Shawn thing, just waved. Just as they both began leaving the parking lot and merging with traffic, a call came out.

"Adam 5, report of possible drug activity involving a white male wearing a leather coat and a red shirt at the corner of Cherry Street and Sixty-Fourth Avenue."

"Adam 5, ten-four, en route."

The call was only about a block from the 7-Eleven and still in Pat's patrol sector. An unmarked narcotics unit radioed that he would take the call as lead unit and that he was responding as well. Pat thought to himself, *Finally, a little bit of fun.* He radioed that he and Capstone were in the area and would back up the unmarked unit.

He turned off his headlights and drove around the corner to the area in which the activity had been reported. A white male wearing a red shirt and a leather jacket was handing another male a small brown bottle that resembled those used for prescriptions.

He advised dispatch that there was activity in the area and that he had just observed a drug transaction go down. Capstone pulled in behind his cruiser just as the male who was holding the brown plastic bottle spotted his unit. The man's expression went from satisfaction to horror. The suspect threw the bottle onto the ground and began to sprint for the nearest alleyway. The other suspect, who was wearing the leather jacket and red shirt, looked at the bottle and then turned toward both police cruisers.

When Capstone and Pat turned on their emergency lights and started pulling toward him, the suspect quickly scooped up the brown bottle and ran toward a newer model Chevy Impala. The engine roared to life and the lights came on instantly. The suspect floored his Impala and quickly turned the vehicle into the path of an oncoming car. Although he swerved, it was too late. The Impala struck the rear corner panel of the oncoming car, causing an explosion of metal and plastic.

The impact pushed the oncoming vehicle out of the Impala's escape route and onto the sidewalk. The driver of the oncoming car looked shocked but gave the officers the thumbs-up sign to show that he was uninjured. This was no longer just a drug bust. The suspect had crossed that invisible line: he had just risked someone's life to keep his freedom. Pat and Capstone decided they were not going to let this asshole enjoy that freedom for much longer.

They quickly caught up to the Impala and radioed its registration plate number to the dispatcher.

"Adam 5 and Adam 6 in pursuit of a newer blue Chevy Impala, Maryland registration Eight–Kilo–Mike–three-one-three-one with heavy front-end damage. Unknown number of occupants; operator was involved in a drug transaction and fled the scene, striking another vehicle, and kept on traveling south on Church Street," relayed Pat.

"Ten-four, Adam 5. All units, Adam 5 and 6 are in pursuit of a newer blue Impala, traveling south on Church Street. Suspect is wanted for leaving the scene of an accident and possible drug activity. Assisting units identify, all non-pursuit units switch over to channel two."

The switch to channel two, one of the backup channels, was so that only units involved in the chase could be involved in the dialogue.

The chase continued down Church Street, and it became evident from the vehicle's swerving back and forth that the driver was having trouble keeping the now damaged Impala traveling in a straight line. The Impala's driver would have to turn onto Fifteenth Street due to road construction on a bridge, which became the opportunity Capstone and Pat had been waiting for.

"Adam 5 to Adam 10, request authorization to ram the suspect's vehicle in order to stop him. Suspect is driving in a reckless manner that is endangering the public," radioed Capstone.

"Adam 10 to Adam 5, permission granted. Be careful. Also be advised, I'm en route to your general vicinity."

"Adam 5 to Adam 6, since you have a bumper bar on your cruiser you'll have to use your cruiser to pin this guy. Pass the guy on the right next chance you get and pin him against the Jersey barrier on the left and I'll block him in from the rear. He won't be able to go anywhere."

"Adam 6, understood."

THE Impala made its clumsy turn onto Fifteenth Street, and it all happened in under a second. It was like Capstone and Pat had practiced the unorthodox maneuver a million times. Pat observed Capstone pass him on the right side. As the Impala just began to turn, Capstone's cruiser struck the front end of the Impala, pushing it into the Jersey barrier. Pat pulled directly behind the Impala at an angle.

They exited their vehicles with guns drawn, and it became evident at that point why the suspect was unable to properly control the vehicle: Both air bags had gone off, making it almost impossible to drive the car, not to mention that the car had been filled with smoke from the air bag deployment. The suspect's hands appeared out of the smoke and he emerged from the smoking cabin with his hands in the air saying, "You guys are freaking out of your mind, you could've killed me! I'm suing your whole department; that was dangerous!"

Pat ordered the man to the ground as Capstone came in with his still-shiny pair of Smith & Wesson handcuffs, handling the man as gently as he had struck that oncoming car. The suspect was getting out of control even in the handcuffs. He continued to proclaim his innocence, even when Sergeant Durkin came on-scene and tried to calm him down. Sergeant Durkin took custody of the suspect momentarily, and his demeanor went from loud and boisterous to that of a whimpering little puppy very fast. Just then the unmarked narcotics officer rolled up on-scene. As he got out of his vehicle and saw who the suspect was, he just shook his head and said, "Poof, you at it again? Search him and the vehicle thoroughly. Our friend here has been known to carry a gun when he's working."

"I'll do the search for drugs and weapons in the vehicle," Hank offered.

"In the meantime, you're going into the back of my cruiser after I search you, dude," Pat said as he took the suspect by the arm and placed him up against the cruiser.

He did the usual body search and came up with some marijuana in the right front pants pocket of the suspect.

"That's another charge, guy," Pat said.

"Bingo!" Hank cried out. "We got a fully loaded .380 Walther PPK under the front driver's seat."

With that the suspect sighed and lowered his gaze to the pavement.

"Well, that will get you a mandatory five-year federal sentence, now won't it?" the narcotics officer asked.

The armed drug dealer did not respond.

Hank and Pat arrived at the station and presented the suspect to the booking sergeant, who clearly had been on the job for a long time. Out of the blue and without so much as touching the suspect, the sergeant asked the man, "You shoot up today?"

"I never touch the stuff."

"Buddy, I've been doing this since you were in diapers, and if you don't have at least one needle or burn mark on your arms or hands, I'll quit my job right now."

The sergeant then pulled the man's jacket down from the shoulders and over the guy's handcuffs, rolled up his sleeves, and there it was: a fresh track mark from a needle, with dried blood around it.

"Right. You never touch the stuff, huh?" the sergeant laughed.

Hank and Pat just shook their heads in amazement. They hoped that one day they would have the experience to just look at a guy and know what he had done. Pat's job skills, unlike his bedroom skills, were still being learned.

As Capstone and Pat left the booking area, Pat saw Sergeant Durkin walking back toward the shift command office and asked to speak with him. The sergeant told Pat he would meet him in the squad room after he was able to ask the narc something in private.

Sergeant Durkin entered the squad room and gave Pat a nod and said, "Why aren't you getting that report done? You do know the narc guy's gonna screw you, leaving you with all of the paperwork? Then he's going to show up just to take the glory and credit for the bust, right?"

"Well, I am the new guy; it happens."

There was one thing he had to ask Sergeant Durkin. In police work everyone seemed to have one specialty or skill that they honed and were able to use as if it were a martial arts weapon. Some guys were expert marksmen, shooting with the precision of a surgeon with a scalpel; some guys could look at someone and size them up in a second, like the sergeant in booking. Sergeant Durkin seemed to have a subtle way with words, and Pat wanted to learn how he did it.

"Sarge," he said, "how'd you get that guy to shut up?"

Walking toward his office, Sergeant Durkin smiled and said, "I advised him of his right to remain silent, and then I advised him to use it, otherwise his rights wouldn't be the only thing I violated."

He knew the sergeant wasn't telling him the whole story, but that would have to do because he closed the door to the command office after shooting Pat a smile and a wink.

He walked around the squad room chuckling at the sergeant's comment and the visions he had of the suspect being "advised" to remain silent. Capstone reentered the squad room; it was now empty except for the two of them. Hank sat down after grabbing two cups of warm stale coffee from the countertop.

Pat then turned his attention to the large stack of reports he had to finish. It wouldn't be too hard, considering he was still floating from the excitement of a drug bust.

After two and a half hours, the narc detective finally showed up to "help" with the paperwork. Pat didn't say anything snide to the detective. A detective outranked a patrolman. Even though Pat was a bit annoyed, he bit his lip and said, "I'm almost done with the paperwork. Wanna look it over?"

The detective grabbed his large stack of paperwork and read it over carefully.

"Good work," he said, as he made a few notes. "Just correct those few things and it's good to go."

He then got up from his seat and said, "Let me know when the hearing is," and walked out of the squad room.

Capstone watched the door until the narc detective got through the doorway and then said to Pat, "Guess rank has its privileges."

He was nearing the end of what turned out to be an exciting shift. Pat grabbed all the necessary reports and took them to the shift commander to be turned in. Sergeant Durkin was in his office. The door was now open and the narc detective was just coming out of the command office as Pat walked down the hallway.

"Hey Sarge, here's everything; the incident report, pursuit report, use of force report, evidence log, vehicle towing card, the arrest report, rap sheet, and finally, the bail sheet." The sergeant looked at Pat and said, "It ain't all cops and robbers, ten minutes of fun and three hours of paperwork. The detective that was on this bust with you is a lieutenant in the narcotics bureau. He was very impressed at how you and Capstone took that guy down. He came in here to give you two a pat on the back."

Pat smiled and thanked the sergeant. "Goodnight, Sarge," he said, and headed home to Dean as another work week came to a close.

Chapter Six
Fishing

THE next day, Hank called Pat around two o'clock in the afternoon, giddy as a schoolgirl.

"Hey, Pat, I called that Shawn and we've got a date!"

Pat was astonished but really happy for Capstone. "When is this big date?" he asked.

"Tonight. Could you and Dean come with us? I'm a little nervous."

Pat remembered mentioning that he would go on a double date with Capstone and one of his tricks.

"I'll have to check with Dean and make sure he's up for it. Where do you want to go?"

"How does dinner and then the club sound?"

Pat loved going to the clubs, especially for the dancing. He didn't want to let on so he played with Capstone a little bit. "I don't know, man. All those people, the loud music!"

Capstone picked up on his sarcasm and said, "Stop, I've seen you at the clubs before, and you're a dancing queen!"

He laughed and said, "Yeah, yeah, whatever, stud. Let me check with Dean and I'll get back to you."

"Okay, let me know as soon as possible so I know what I'm doing."

"Will do. Now calm down," he said with a laugh.

Dean would be home in a couple of hours and Pat figured he wouldn't mind going out with Hank and Shawn, especially if he cooked for once and made something nice. He hoped that this thing with Shawn would work out for Hank, as he knew he had been a little lonely in his personal life. Time would tell, and he certainly wouldn't mind having that cute little fucker show up once in a while.

As the door opened, Dean flew in and Pat grabbed him and kissed him like the world was ending. When he broke loose from his death grip, Pat saw the big smile on Dean's face.

"What was that all about?"

"Nothing special. I was just thinking about you all day and couldn't wait for you to get home, sweetheart."

"You know the sweetest things to say to me. What do you want?" Dean asked with a smirk.

"Nothing, just wanted you in my arms, that's all," Pat said with a big smile.

"Well, that *is* sweet of you."

"Now come sit down because I want to ask you something."

"Oh no, now what? I knew you were up to something."

"Nothing bad. Just that Hank wants us to double date with him tonight with a new guy he is hooking up with. He's a little nervous and wants us as a security blanket, that's all."

"What did you have in mind?"

"Well, Hank suggested dinner and the club. What do you think?"

"Yeah, that's cool, as long as we aren't out too late. I have a big day at the office tomorrow with a government bank auditor, and I don't want to be falling asleep while he's talking."

"Great. I'll let Hank know. By the way, I made dinner, just in case you didn't want to go out, so we'll save it for tomorrow night."

"Sounds good. What did you make?"

"Nothing special. I just made a sauce for tortellini, which will age overnight now and be all the better for it."

They all met at Isabella's restaurant for dinner. They loved the place. It was one of those small chic restaurants that varied their menu every two or three months to coincide with the change of seasons. They found a small candlelit table in the corner where they knew they wouldn't be disturbed or overheard. The manager knew Dean and Pat well and so there was no problem getting the table they wanted.

Pat had never seen Capstone dressed up before. He wore a tight pair of Abercrombie & Fitch khakis and a dark blue button-down Versace shirt. It was quite obvious that Hank was trying very hard to impress Shawn, and Pat couldn't blame him.

Shawn had done his part too. His black hair was spiked short, his smooth face was clean-shaven, and he had splashed on his favorite cologne, Calvin Klein for men. With the face and body that Shawn possessed, he could have easily been an Abercrombie & Fitch model. His clothes showed he had uncommon good taste in style for someone so young. He was wearing gray cargo pants with a red polo shirt, which showed that this boy worked out. His perfect chest was highlighted from under the shirt and the short red sleeves were barely able to contain the two mounds of bicep. He certainly looked much better than when he stood behind the 7-Eleven counter wearing that funky apron.

Pat couldn't help himself as he stared at Shawn; he now looked at this boy quite differently. He was no longer just a source of free coffee but someone who had great sex appeal, as well as someone special to his police partner. Dean apparently noticed Pat's enthrallment with Shawn, as he kicked his lover under the table and brought Pat back to Earth quickly.

Pat watched how Capstone and Shawn interacted throughout dinner. Capstone was a bit reserved and quiet, while Shawn talked a lot about school and how he was working on his bachelor's in accounting from the University of Maryland. Pat ordered the Maryland cream of crab soup and Dean had a steak cooked rare like he always did. His man always did love large chunks of meat. No wonder he loved Pat!

They skipped the dessert and decided to head out to the club. Shawn wanted to go to one of his normal hangouts near the college. Pat had been there once in his wilder days but Dean said he had never heard of the place, so it would be a new experience.

They piled into Pat's private car and he drove to the club. When they arrived, Shawn noted that the place had changed a little, but there were still tons of hot college guys floating around the front of the building. Now, unlike before, there was a big neon sign proclaiming the name of the bar to be "The Closet."

The parking lot was as full as Pat had expected, even on a week night. After a long, hard day of classes, the boys came here to play and have fun. Pat held Dean's hand as they walked into the front doorway of the club and Capstone and Shawn followed.

They had that awkward first-date air about them, the kind where you're not sure if you should hold hands or touch on the shoulder, fearing that the other person might get the wrong idea.

From the reputation of this place and from what a few friends had told him, The Closet was more of a meat market than a club. He was thinking Shawn might be willing to do a bit more than hold hands on the first date. Rumor had it that the backroom floor of this place had more seed on it than a farmer's field. Pat didn't share that little tidbit of information.

Instead, he just smiled and listened to the familiar beat from the house music before rubbing himself up against Dean to let him know that it was time to hit the dance floor. As they split off from Capstone and Shawn, they let them know they were going to dance and Pat winked at Capstone, giving him a look that said "good luck." He wanted to give them a little alone time to relate in a more intimate environment.

Shaun and Hank headed upstairs to a bar that was set aside for the boys who don't dance or for those who actually wanted to talk to their tricks before heading to the backroom or home.

AFTER about a half-hour of dancing, Pat and Dean had worked up a sweat from grinding and dry-humping on the dance floor. Pat had to yell to Dean to be heard above the music.

"Hey, stud, wanna go upstairs and get to know your trick before we hook up?"

Dean just shook his head and smiled.

"Naw, I just wanna use you up and go home to the husband," he shot back.

They both laughed and he grabbed Dean's sweaty muscular shoulders. He was so hard he could have ripped off his clothes right there and fucked him on the dance floor. In this place, probably no one would have noticed. He turned Dean around and led him off of the dance floor to the stairway leading up to the quiet bar, pushing his raging hard-on into his butt the whole time.

They walked into the bar and saw Shawn and Hank with a round of untouched drinks in front of them. They were kissing passionately in a corner booth. They had quite the audience too, even though it wasn't an uncommon occurrence in a gay bar to have two men kissing. In this case, it was two unbelievably hot men making out hot and heavy.

Dean and Pat looked at each other and smiled. Pat grabbed Dean and pushed him against the wall, deciding to make it a double feature for all of the voyeurs in the peanut gallery.

Shawn and Hank must have spotted their friends after about ten minutes or so because Capstone came up behind Pat and cleared his throat loudly while tapping him on the shoulder.

"Knock it off, you two. You're making the rest of us nauseous! Two old married men doing that in public!" he laughed.

Pat disengaged his tongue from Dean's mouth and looked at Capstone.

"Sorry, just figured your date was going so badly, that we'd let you two alone for a little longer. Besides, he heard two studs were putting on a show up here and he just had to see it for himself."

Capstone blushed and Shawn just chuckled. He couldn't help but notice that Shawn had sprouted a tent in his trousers. Pat looked at Dean and said, "I'll be right back. I gotta take a leak."

He knew that would be a feat in itself if his hard-on didn't fade soon. He walked into the men's room of The Closet. As he turned toward the urinal he felt uneasy, as if someone was standing behind him.

The hairs on the back of his neck stood on end and a giant knot began to form in his stomach. Pat turned around and saw him standing there and smiling with an arrogant, look-what-I-found look on his face.

It was the guy from the drug bust the other day. He wasn't dressed much better than the day the department had arrested him. Pat tried not to acknowledge him. He turned back around to piss. It was too late; he knew the guy had seen and recognized him. He moved into the urinal next to Pat and said, "Quite the show you and your buddy were putting on out there." He looked down at Pat's cock and then his own and asked, "See anything you like?"

Pat didn't acknowledge him verbally He wasn't sure how to handle the situation. Was he in danger? Was the guy armed? What did he want?

The suspect looked over at Pat as he continued to do his business and said, "You guys took my old cell phone so I got this new one. It has video and picture capability. It's really nice; the quality is high too."

The dirtball put his dick away and zipped his fly and started to wash his hands. Pat was frozen in fear of the implied threat of being outed at work. He didn't want the man next to him to know that he was afraid, but an animal like this could smell the type of fear he was emitting. Pat could take the danger of guns, high-speed chases, and the diseases he constantly encountered; those were risks he was prepared to take. But how would the guys at work handle his being gay? Would he have to give up the job he loved and move away?

The guy finished washing his hands and walked over to the stalls, looking into each one. Pat zipped up, patted his left inner waistband to make sure he was armed, and started to wash his hands. The guy began to speak again.

"Like you guys said, that gun is gonna get me federal time, and I don't need the headache of the other charges. I think you made a mistake."

He could tell where this was going and he should have grabbed that son of a bitch by the throat and slammed him off of every wall from here to the door, but he didn't; the fear of his colleagues knowing he was gay was too overpowering. This slime ball, this scumbag, had power over Pat, and he knew it.

Pat couldn't find the words to tell the dirtbag off, as his throat was closed and his mouth was dry. The man had the smile of the Cheshire cat, knowing he was getting through to the cop.

"Here's how this works. If my charges get tossed for an error on the arresting officer's part, my phone accidentally gets erased and this ten-minute video of you and Barney Fife never gets sent to your departmental e-mail account or anyone else." He paused to let that sink in. "However, what do I have to lose if I'm going to prison for a long time anyway? And as a bonus, I'll even let you suck my cock."

"No thanks. I don't eat snacks."

"And if you're thinking, why don't you just take the cell phone from my hand, I'll warn you now that I have already e-mailed photos of both of you locked in a deep, wet, gay kiss," he said with a laugh.

The man then did something he couldn't believe. At the time he wasn't sure why he did it, but the dirtball took out an eight ball of cocaine and snorted a line right off the countertop. The cop in Pat was screaming to bust him, to kick him, to do anything but stand there feeling helpless.

Just then a couple of college boys opened the door to the bathroom, looked at the man who was putting away his kit, and said, "Hey, Floyd."

Pat looked at him. "Your name's not Floyd."

The man just laughed and in an excited voice said, "Man, you *are* a rookie. My street name's 'Pink Floyd' or 'Poof' as in 'poofter', 'cuz I'm gay like you, you dumbass. Only difference is my people don't care who or what I fuck, long as I hook them up."

Pat backed away from the man and walked out of the bathroom in a daze. He was very angry with himself. He was trained to deal with life-and-death situations every day as a cop, but this guy was able to disarm him with one sentence. His head was spinning. *What should I do?* It would be easy to screw up the case at the preliminary hearing. If he did, the video would never come to light, or so "Floyd" had said. He walked out to the quiet bar and Dean could immediately tell something was wrong.

"What's wrong, Pat?"

"Just saw someone I don't like in the bathroom and he kinda rattled me a bit. I'll be okay." Capstone gave Pat the look a fellow cop gives another cop when he knows he isn't telling the whole truth or something is really wrong. He let it go without another word, for the moment.

They'd been sitting in the booth for about twenty minutes when Capstone said, "I'm not feeling so good, and I think we should go."

Shawn looked disappointed and asked Capstone if he was sure he had to go. Capstone said "Yeah, but I will call you later. I promise."

They all piled back into Pat's car as Hank and Shawn talked a little bit more. Dean and Pat were silent. They headed to Shawn's house first; before he got out of the car he gave Capstone a kiss and said, "Talk to you later, stud." The rest of the ride was pretty quiet. As Pat pulled into Capstone's driveway, he gave him a look that was meant to communicate that he needed to talk to him right away.

Dean caught on and said, "Okay, what's going on? Hank's not sick and he doesn't believe you told me everything about what happened in the bathroom."

He asked Hank to get out of the car and told him he'd talk to him in a second.

"Dean, when I went to the bathroom I saw a guy who we arrested last week. He threatened to out me and Capstone if we don't dismiss the charges."

Dean looked worried. "See, this is what I meant about the dangers of this job."

Pat looked lovingly at Dean and said, "Dean, please don't. There's enough going on in my head right now. Dean, I love you and I want to tell you everything that happens in my life, but please let me work this thing out, okay?"

When Dean got out of the car he wasn't sure if he was angry, worried, or hurt. Maybe it was all of the above. He decided they would have to have a long talk about sharing and how important it would be for them.

Pat motioned for Capstone to get back into the car.

"We have a little bit of a problem," he said.

Capstone looked at him and said, "If this is about how I acted in the bar—"

Pat cut him off midsentence, as this issue was too important and his chest felt like it was going to explode if he didn't get it out immediately.

"In the men's room at the club, I ran into that dirtbag we arrested on the drug bust. He's going to out us if we don't drop the charges."

Capstone leaned back a little bit and cocked his head. "What do you mean? How?" he asked.

"When you and I were making out with Dean and Shawn, the guy was videoing the whole thing."

Capstone's hand went to his forehead and he exclaimed loudly, "Fuck, are you sure he videoed it? I mean, did you see the video?" Capstone asked, his voice oozing with anxiety.

Pat looked out the windshield of the car thinking for a second. He looked at Capstone and said, "I don't know. I mean, he had a cell phone with a camera. I saw that much, and he was there. Are we willing to risk it?"

Capstone punched the dashboard and exclaimed "Fuck!" again. After a few seconds of tense silence, Capstone asked, "What should we do?"

Pat looked at Capstone with his eyes wide open, his chest pounding, and his head spinning, and said, "I'm not sure. I have to think about this." With that, Capstone got out of the car and left without saying a word

As Pat and Dean drove home, Dean placed his hand on Pat's leg in a gesture of concern and love. Pat remained silent and Dean didn't push for any answers. When they got home and Pat pulled into the driveway, Dean got out and headed into the house.

Pat sat in the driver's seat of his car with the motor running and decided he needed to go for a ride. He turned off his cell phone and drove. He decided to drive into Washington DC; the city was beautiful at night with all of the monuments lit up and it would help distract him for a while.

He had so many things to think about. *Why had he become a cop in the first place? How come he didn't just deck the guy and smash his cell phone? What would he tell Dean? If he did what the scumbag wanted, how could he live with himself as a cop or even as a person?*

He turned on the radio for a little bit of background noise while he thought; he found some station playing some 1980s classic rock. It was Laura Branigan, and while he may have had a lot to think about, Pat felt a need to listen to dance music.

One of his main concerns was that the guys at the station would find out his little secret and lose respect for him, or worse, not back him up when he needed it.

In the macho world of police, it didn't matter to some guys how many people you saved or what you did for them. You could be a SWAT cop super stud, but if they found out you sucked a little cock or liked to fuck guys you would become a virtual pariah to many of the cops. Pat suspected it was merely their own personal insecurities scaring them, not the fear that he'd actually try to fuck any of them.

As he drove past the World War II memorial that was just built, he decided to pull over. He took his .380 automatic off-duty weapon back out of the glove compartment where he had stored it after leaving the bar and put it in his off-duty holster. This was not a city in which a person should walk around alone at night unarmed. It was early in the morning. Three a.m., to be exact.

He took a stroll around the WWII monument. It was a huge marble plaza with a fountain in the center with all of the states listed on bronze plaques affixed on the walls around the memorial.

A park police officer walked up to him and said, "Hey, the monuments are closed at night. What are you doing here?" He pulled out his badge and showed him he was on the job as well. The cop told him to not stay too long and Pat thanked him and walked away.

He got back into his car and pulled off. He knew no matter how long he drove around or what he did to avoid the talk he would be having with Dean when he got home, it was inevitable.

He drove back toward home and got in around six a.m., feeling a little less anxious and stressed than he had before his drive. Dean was up and waiting for him.

"Pat, where have you been? I've been worried sick about you!"

"Sorry, honey, but I just had to get out and clear my head and try to solve this problem."

"But Pat, if you don't let me all the way in, I can't help you with this or any other problem that comes up between us or against us."

"I know, Dean, but this is a police problem and I don't want to burden you with it."

"Pat, you are the one that said you are more than just a guy employed as a cop, that you are a cop inside and out. If you don't let me in there to help, then I can't be a part of your whole life! Is that what you want?"

"No. Of course not, Dean. I trust you with anything that is mine or about me."

"Good, then let's talk about this. What exactly did he say?"

"Okay. He tried to blackmail me. Said that if I didn't screw up his criminal case so that he got away with it and the case was dismissed, he would e-mail the video of the two of us, as well as Hank and Shawn kissing at the bar, to the department. He believes that this would be disastrous for my career and he might be right!"

"So, what do you plan on doing, fuck up the case so that he goes away?"

"I'm still trying to work it all out, and it has to be done in conjunction with Hank as he's caught up in this too and has just as much to lose as I do."

"I'm tired. Let's go to bed and deal with this more after a few hours of sleep. I'm calling off tomorrow, or should I say today?" said Dean.

As they went upstairs Pat's mind was working overtime, but he thought Dean was right. Sleep was needed to help clear the mind. As they got into bed, Dean threw his arm over Pat's chest and held him close, whispering, "I love you, no matter what you decide to do."

Pat was very moved by this beautiful man who had come to mean so much to him. Looking at him in the dim light of the sunrise, his cock grew hard despite the rotten night before. They made love, not the slow, tender all-consuming type of love, but the fast, furious kind meant to release stress and to feel a quick bolt of pleasure. He fucked Dean hard and quick and when he came, he rolled over to catch his breath and he heard Dean whisper, "Now go to sleep, my love."

HIS weekend was over and it was time to return to work. He came into the station and found a hearing notice for the drug suspect in his mailbox. The hearing was set for two days from now; Pat and Hank had one night to choose what path they would take.

Since Hank and Pat worked the same schedule, Hank was on as well. They met up but avoided the 7-Eleven that night. They needed to have a serious talk about what was happening. Capstone's cruiser pulled up under the bridge next to Pat's. It had turned rather windy, and there was a light mist in the air. They both rolled down their driver's side windows, and Pat asked, "Hey, how's it going, Hank?"

"Lousy. I didn't sleep very well the last two nights," he replied.

"I can understand that."

Capstone told Pat that Shawn had called him the next day to make sure everything was okay. Capstone told him he would see him for coffee the first night back. He said Shawn was pleased with that answer and assured Hank he would have free doughnuts for both officers to go with his special coffee. They chatted a little longer about their relationships and finally got into the meat of the matter.

"I can't do it," Pat said.

"Do what?" Capstone asked.

"I got into this line of work to help people and I knew there would be sacrifices. I mean, we are supposed to be willing to lay down our lives to enforce the law; how can we turn our backs on that responsibility? If we let one scumbag drug dealer have the power to do this to us, where do we stop? Who knows if he will tell the other dealers this information, and they all start pulling this little trick?"

"Well, let's take that power away from him," he replied.

"Hank," he said sternly, "are you telling me we are just going to let this guy out us? You know what will happen to us?"

Capstone asked, "Well, what's the alternative?"

He looked at Capstone and said, "You're right. If we let him out us, we are probably finished as cops. If we throw the case and get him out of this, we are either lousy cops or crooked cops and we might get fired anyway."

Capstone added, "We could also get arrested for playing those types of games too."

"Well, he could always be found floating in the Anacostia River now, can't he? He would be just another victim of the new killer."

"Pat! 'Course, now there's a thought," Hank said as they both laughed.

They talked for about another ten minutes and came up with a plan of action. It wasn't going to be easy, but they decided to out themselves so if that video showed up it wouldn't be a surprise to anyone. They weren't going to let the behind-the-back whispers start; they were going to deal with this thing head-on. There really wasn't any other choice.

At the end of the shift they walked into the stationhouse and found the rest of the shift standing down as well. The oncoming shift was in roll call.

Sergeant Durkin was in his command office briefing the incoming shift sergeant. The narcotics lieutenant from the drug bust was also in the office. Pat decided to wait until the narcotics lieutenant left the office to try to talk to Durkin.

As Capstone and Pat finished putting their shotguns back in the armory, the narcotics lieutenant walked up behind Pat and tapped him on the shoulder.

"I need to talk to you about the arrest the other night," he said.

"Okay, lieutenant. Right now? I need to see Sergeant Durkin really quick if that's okay?" he said, hoping the lieutenant wouldn't start pulling rank or thinking Pat was being dismissive in some way. Pat was tense, and it had taken him hours to build up the courage to do what he knew needed to be done. The lieutenant replied, "Okay, but make sure you come see me right after. I'm leaving in a half-hour."

He walked into Sergeant Durkin's office just as he was putting on his jacket and getting ready to leave for the day.

"That narcotics lieutenant is looking for you," he said, without making eye contact with his star rookie.

"Yeah, I saw him before he came in here. I have to talk to you about something rather important."

The sergeant asked, "Okay. What's up?"

Pat looked at him, almost unable to make eye contact, and asked if he could close the door so they could speak freely. Durkin took off his jacket and offered him a seat.

"What's on your mind?" he asked, with genuine concern in his voice.

Pat didn't think he should beat around the bush. "I'm being blackmailed," he said matter-of-factly.

The sergeant didn't seem too surprised; the statement barely got a reaction out of him. He just raised his eyebrow and asked, "Capstone too?"

Pat could barely breathe and he felt a little nauseous. "Yeah, Sarge. How'd you know?"

"I've been doing this job for many years and I'm good at reading people. Don't you wonder why I let Capstone back you up without question any time you radio for backup?"

He sat there waiting for him to say the word he felt was coming; the word he thought would hit so hard it would knock him out. In his mind he kept repeating, *Say it, Sarge. Say you know we're gay, say it so I don't have to.* He didn't think he could utter the words if he wanted to.

The sergeant said one more thing to Pat before he put his jacket back on and left the office for the day. "The only way to beat a blackmailer is to take away the power they have over you. It's not easy, but what's the alternative? You know what you have to do, so do it."

"Understood, Sarge."

"Don't forget, the lieutenant is waiting for you," he said as he left the office.

As he walked upstairs to the narcotics lieutenant's office, he wondered how long Sergeant Durkin had known. He didn't seem too disturbed about Pat's being gay. He didn't even seem too disturbed about Pat and Hank being blackmailed, come to think of it. They didn't even cover who was blackmailing him or any of the specifics. What the hell had just happened in there?

The lieutenant was sitting at his desk when Pat opened the door. He told Pat to take a seat and offered him a Diet Coke. The lieutenant didn't even wait for Pat to start speaking. He tapped on a fish tank he kept in his office and said, "I love fish. Watching them calms me down after a high-stress day. Today was a high-stress day. Some knucklehead drug dealer got stabbed when a deal went bad and he asked for me by name as he lay dying on a gurney."

Pat looked at the lieutenant, wondering where he was going with this.

"I also keep them in my office to remind me that as police officers, we live in a fishbowl every day," he said as he fed his fish and watched the fish swim about eating the flakes he was pouring into the water.

Pat was tired from the long night shift and the effects of the attempted blackmail, and this wasn't helping. It wasn't like he hadn't heard all of this before in the police academy. One instructor would always remind the rookies that they were under constant surveillance like a fish in a fishbowl; every little move and swish was observed by the public.

The lieutenant sat back down in his worn swivel desk chair and looked him in the eye. "I've watched you work ever since the gay-bar bombings. You seem to have the instincts to be a good cop; just not the experience yet. You'll do well, I'm sure."

The lieutenant continued to speak without pause. "This isn't the most tolerant department I've ever worked in and I can understand how that can play on someone's mind, making them feel vulnerable."

Pat's gut tightened up, as he knew where he was going with this.

"Lieutenant," he interrupted.

The lieutenant straightened up in his chair and his face took on a light shade of pink as he said in an elevated voice that was not quite yelling, "I'm not finished, St. James, and do not interrupt me again."

Pat jumped back a little bit in his seat; the lieutenant had changed from a grandpa-type mentor to commanding officer in a matter of seconds.

"Our drug dealer from the other night got himself stabbed twelve times in a drug deal gone bad. It seems he lost his gun somewhere and the assailant took advantage of that fact."

The lieutenant opened his desk drawer and pulled out a very familiar-looking cell phone, which was covered in blood. "Just before our friend died he mumbled something about Patrolmen St. James and Capstone being in a video that was saved on his phone."

This was the moment Pat had dreaded since he had decided to become a cop; someone finally, without a doubt, knew he was gay. Not only that but the same person had watched him ramming his tongue down some guy's throat and grabbing his cock. And of all people, it had to be brass that found out.

He sunk down in his seat and covered his face in fear. It was out: Everyone was going to know Capstone and Pat were gay. Their careers were over.

The lieutenant put the phone on the desk and pushed it toward him. Just the sight of the phone made Pat sick. It wasn't the blood or gore on the phone; it was what was in the phone. That stupid video!

The lieutenant leaned way back in his swivel chair and said, "St. James, there is nothing illegal about what you did; but you have to remember in public, on duty and off, someone is always watching."

The lieutenant flipped the phone open to the screen with the video stills and sure enough there he was right up against Dean, fully engaged in a hot, deep kiss.

"There are a lot of assholes on this job that would run you right out of this department because they think you'd be a threat to their manhood, or that you can't do the job."

Pat took his hands away from his face and looked the lieutenant square in the eyes and said, "The suspect was going to blackmail me over this video. He saw me in the bar that night and told me that if I didn't drop the charges he would get that video out to every cop he could find."

"Well," the lieutenant asked, "what was your plan? Don't bullshit me. Were you or Capstone going to drop the charges or sabotage the case?"

He looked at the lieutenant and shook his head side to side slowly.

"Lieutenant, it crossed my mind for about twenty minutes, but Capstone and I couldn't go through with it. That was the reason I asked you if I could see Sergeant Durkin first before coming up here. I stopped in to tell him everything."

The lieutenant said, "I wouldn't worry about the dealer anymore. He died of his wounds about two hours ago."

Pat looked at the still image on the phone once more and then back at the lieutenant and asked, "Did anyone else see the video?"

"No, but Sergeant Durkin knows what was going on, because I told him to send you to me and that I would deal with this."

The lieutenant then picked up the phone and removed the memory chip.

"I asked the dealer if he sent the video to anyone yet and he said not yet and that's why he asked for me. He figured since I was narcotics that I was some macho asshole that would fuck your day up."

The lieutenant tossed the chip at Pat and said, "Put that somewhere that you will see it every day. I want it to remind you that someone's always watching, everything you do and say."

Pat snapped up the chip as fast as he could and put it in his pocket. He cocked his head a little bit, not fully understanding what was going on. He wondered if this was it; was the lieutenant going to let him off that easy? Would he actually not tell anyone? He realized he didn't care; the blackmailer was dead, he had the video, and only the lieutenant, Sergeant Durkin, Capstone, and he knew of the incident.

"Lieutenant, if I may be blunt. Are you going to tell anyone what you saw on that cell phone? Do I have to worry about the other guys finding out about Capstone and me?"

"The only people you have to worry about letting the department know are you and Capstone. As for me, how can I tell anyone about something that exists on a tiny memory chip that I don't have and never saw? Your private life is your business as far as I am concerned. Do your job and never turn your back on the job. That's what I care about. Who knows? Maybe one day you will be working for me in narcotics."

As he got up and started to walk out of the lieutenant's office, something didn't feel right.

"Lieutenant, are you sure it's okay if I keep this chip? Isn't it evidence in a murder? Won't his family want it back?"

The lieutenant simply looked at Pat in a puzzled fashion as he put his jacket on to leave and said, "What chip? What are you talking about?"

With that he walked out of his office door and down the hallway.

Pat ran down to the squad room and found that Capstone was still sitting there waiting for him.

"Where did you go, man?" he asked. "I thought we were going to talk to Sergeant Durkin about the blackmail thing. I can't do this alone, man."

Pat looked at Capstone and showed him the little blue chip and said, "Hearing's canceled. Suspect was killed in a drug deal gone bad."

Capstone had the look of a deer caught in headlights. "What are you saying, Pat?"

Pat put his hand on Capstone's shoulder and said, "Lieutenant Farrell from narcotics saw the video and knows. Sergeant Durkin didn't see the video but knows we are gay. We are free and clear; no one is ever going to see this video and none of the cops are going to know about our little secret."

Just then two other officers from the day shift walked into the squad room to get some coffee. Pat looked at Capstone and said he needed to stop by a pet store.

"I have an overwhelming desire to buy a pet fish."

Chapter Seven
Let the Games Begin

As Hank walked around his one-bedroom apartment waiting for the game to come on, he looked for something to do. The phone rang, relieving him of that duty.

"Hello?"

"Hi, stud, Shawn here."

"Hi, yourself, cutie. Nice to hear your voice. What's going on?" Hank asked as his mind began to conjure up all sorts of things.

"Thought I would give you a call and see what you're doing tonight. I was hoping maybe you and I could get together, you know, just the two of us?"

"Ah, I couldn't think of a thing I would rather do than spend the evening with you. Why don't we go out for something to eat, and then back to my place and watch a movie or something?"

"Yeah, or something. Sounds like a plan to me. What time should we meet?"

"Why don't you come over around seven, and we'll take it from there?"

"Okay, Hank. See you then!"

After hanging up the phone, Hank jumped into the shower to get ready for his date. For whatever reason, he began to sing some old advertising slogan: "I feel lucky tonight, I feel lucky tonight!"

Right on time, a knock on the door announced the arrival of Shawn and the start of what Hank hoped would be a memorable evening. When he opened the door, he found Shawn standing there in black pants, white shirt, and dress shoes, looking like a million bucks. Shawn gave him a big smile and then a huge hug hello.

"Come in, guy! You look great tonight!"

"I look great every night in case you haven't noticed."

"True, you do look sexy in your little 7-Eleven apron with the coffee stain on the front."

"You're just jealous because you can't pull off the look like I can."

"So, you don't like my police uniform?"

"No, never said that!" Shawn replied with an evil grin. "But I like you out of that uniform as well."

"You know where my uniform would look best?"

"No. Where?"

"On the floor, next to your bed!"

They both laughed at once and headed out the door after Hank got his car keys. They had dinner at one of the many small restaurants that dot the county and were back at the apartment by 9:15.

"Wanna watch a movie?" Hank asked.

"I'd rather watch you fuck me, how about that?"

"Damn, you don't have to ask me twice, sexy. The bedroom is this way."

"Who needs the bedroom, when you have a lovely sofa?"

With that statement, Shawn kicked off his shoes and slowly removed his shirt, revealing his near-perfect chest. A fine line of hair went from his navel down to below the belt.

"Wanna finish the rest, Hank?"

The question knocked Hank out of the trance he had fallen into while watching this beautiful man take off his clothes. Without hesitation, he moved over to Shawn and took off his belt and lowered his zipper. He sat down on the sofa with Shawn standing right in front of him and reached up to pull Shawn's pants down, ever so slowly. Inch by inch, more and more of the treasure trove that was Shawn was revealed. Finally, the pants and underwear came down far enough so that Shawn's cock popped free and bounced up and down directly in front of Hank's lips.

Shawn was now standing naked in his living room, and it only took Hank a minute to join Shawn in the same state of undress. They each now stood looking into the eyes of the other as if trying to see inside each other's souls. Shawn's eyes moved down Hank's tight, rigid body, stopping for a few seconds to gaze upon his equipment.

"Hank, not only are you handsome, but you got some body on you. And your cock! Who would have expected you to be hung like this?"

"Shawn, you are one beautiful boy and if I don't see your ass fast, I'm going to push you over and flip you like a hamburger!"

Shawn broke out laughing and slowly turned to reveal a perfect ass that would have scored a ten across the board in the ass Olympics. It matched the rest of his looks, which made him damn near perfect. *How could I be so lucky?* Hank wondered.

Hank got the correct impression that Shawn wanted him to take control of their lovemaking, and so he did. He moved Shawn down onto the sofa and kissed him deeply with great passion. It had been a long time since he had such a man in his arms and he was going to make the most of it.

Hank slowly began to kiss Shawn on his neck and chest, stopping only to lick and suck on each nipple. Shawn moaned with pleasure as Hank worked on his pecs. He continued down the athletic body with his tongue, tasting each savory inch of his date. When his tongue hit the coarse hair of the pubic region, he could no longer control himself. He dove onto Shawn's cock and took it straight down his throat, resting his chin on Shawn's balls. It cut off his ability to breathe, but he was more than willing to sacrifice a little air for the pleasure he got from taking Shawn all the way.

Shawn let out a moan that was more warning than pleasure, as he felt the beginnings of a climax. "Easy, babe. You're going to make me cum already. You took my cock like Grant took Richmond! Damn, that was good. Now lay back, stud!"

Hank reluctantly gave up his control of Shawn's nicely shaped cock and resigned himself into Shawn's oral care. Shawn quickly proved that he was no virgin either as he expertly ministered to Hank's rigid phallus. Shawn worked his tongue from the tip of his cock, to the bottom of his balls, sucking the shaft only briefly. Shawn did not want this party to end early! Hank could not believe that the cute guy from the 7-Eleven was now on the other end of his dick. His mind drifted to Shawn's most valuable asset, and he almost came then and there.

"Easy, stud, or I'll fill your mouth with pure wholesome creamy goodness."

Shawn laughed so hard, he almost fell off the sofa.

"You know, that's what I like about you. Besides your big fat cop cock, that is; your sense of humor!"

"Yeah, I'm a regular riot. Now suck my cock."

"With pleasure, big boy."

As Shawn began once again to suck and lightly pinch at Hank's nipples, Hank raised a leg and threw it over the sofa back. He was getting fantastic head when Shawn suddenly stopped. As he looked down, he saw that smile again on his new man's face once again.

"What?!"

"Hank, I'm gonna rock your world!"

With that statement, Shawn moved Hank's other leg up in the air, pushing both legs back toward his head. This gymnastic movement fully exposed his asshole, which was immediately covered by Shawn's face. As Shawn worked his tongue in and out of his ass, Hank's head felt like it exploded.

"Oh my Gawd! No one has ever done that before. It's incredible," he blurted out between gasps for air. "Whatever you do, don't stop!"

Shawn smiled inside as he continued his work. He was almost certain by Hank's reaction that no one had ever eaten his ass before and, while Hank was no virgin, Shawn knew that Hank was experiencing a new sexual skill that he would remember for the rest of his life.

After another ten minutes, Shawn came up for air and rolled over onto his stomach, exposing his incredibly well-built ass to the eye-fucking Hank was giving it. As Hank caught his breath, he was unable to take his eyes off what was one of the best asses he had seen in his life, let alone available for anything that would please Hank sexually. Shawn motioned for Hank to move his body over so that he could lie next to Shawn. Hank eagerly complied and began to rub his ass. Shawn's ass was as smooth as silk and practically screamed "Fuck me!"

Hank ran his tongue over each cheek, relishing the texture and feel of this man's ass. He wanted to fully possess the two mounds of flesh in all their glory. Hank briefly thought about returning the favor to Shawn, but rightly decided that he could not do that and not cum. Instead, he rolled Shawn back onto his back and stared directly into the eye of Shawn's cock. Now this he knew how to handle!

He used nothing but his tongue on the cock and balls of his date. He breathed in Shawn's manly scent as he gave close attention to his friend's pleasure. Shawn moaned and wiggled from the expert tonguing that he was being given. Finally, Hank took Shawn's shaft into his mouth and repeatedly went up and down on the prize cock. Shawn's nipples were fully erect as he responded to the massive stimulation that Hank was giving to him. Shawn grabbed the back of his head with both hands, and began to fuck his mouth, thrusting up and down with his hips. Suddenly he stopped, advising Hank that he was getting close. Instead of pulling off of Shawn's cock, he sucked even harder, now determined to drain every ounce of cum out of Shawn's balls.

Shawn arched his back and let out a loud, long growl that filled the apartment as he exploded deep into Hank's mouth, releasing spurt after spurt of hot cum. Hank drank it all in greedily and was careful not to let any spill out of his mouth. He knew that Shawn was finished cumming when he relaxed his back, and the eruptions went still. He swallowed one last time and slowly pulled off of Shawn's cock.

"Damn, that was one fine blow job, Hank! I love it when a guy swallows what I took so much care to make!"

"I couldn't help myself; I had to have it and could not wait any longer. I wanted to taste you, and for you to become part of me. Just jack me off; that's all I need."

"Jack you off, my ass! You get to work on my ass with that tool of yours."

With that, he watched Shawn turn over, shoving his ass into the air slightly. Hank opened up a drawer in the end table and took out lube and a rubber. He worked a generous amount of lube into the waiting asshole of his date as well as all over his engorged cock. He placed a pillow under Shawn's hips so that he could relax and not have to hold his ass up.

"Now just relax, Shawn, and I'll go slowly. Let me know if it hurts."

"Hank, this isn't my first time at the prom, you know?"

"Right, Shawn, but I do have almost ten inches here, and I don't want to hurt you."

"You just fuck, let me worry about taking it."

With that order being given, he began to enter the tight, inviting ass of his date. After his head entered Shawn's ass, he let his cock rest there so that Shawn could relax and take it. No matter what Shawn said, many a guy before him said they could take his cock only to find that they could not. Having to stop always frustrated the hell out of Hank and he really wanted to finish with Shawn.

"Hank, I'm okay. Go on."

With that encouragement, he sunk his cock into Shawn's willing ass much like a hot knife goes through butter. When he was fully inside of Shawn, a feeling of satisfaction washed over him. He began to slowly fuck Shawn with steady in and out strokes. Shawn began to moan and he became worried that once again he was too big to fuck a guy.

"Am I hurting you, Shawn?"

"No, for Gawd's sake, just shut up and fuck me! Fuck me like you mean it!"

That was all the encouragement he needed. He began to pick up steam like a battleship going into ramming speed. He gave Shawn long steady strokes of his cock, which also gave him maximum pleasure. After about five minutes, he flipped Shawn over onto his back, and entered him from the front. This way he was able to look directly into Shawn's beautiful eyes as he fucked the hell out of him.

After another couple of minutes of fucking, he could stand it no more. He was now slamming Shawn so hard that they were inching their way off the sofa. Finally, he bent his head back and hissed, "Fuck, I'm gonna cum!"

"Give it to me, baby! Fuck me good!"

With that being said, he exploded with a rushing stream of cum that traveled down the length of his cock and into the waiting, well-used rubber. He moaned throughout the climax while Shawn twisted his nipples. Finally, he collapsed onto Shawn's chest, fully exhausted for the moment. Both of them were breathing hard until the rise and fall of their chests became one in unison of movement. Little by little, his now softening cock began its march out of the rectum of his new lover. With a final movement, his cock flopped out and onto the sofa cushion. Shawn felt the vacuum left by the exit of Hank's cock and felt empty deep inside his soul.

"That was incredible, Shawn. Thank you."

"You're such a stud, Hank, you don't even know it. That was a mighty good fuck, and I needed it. Lots of guys talk a big game, but honey, you deliver."

"Come on; let's get cleaned up in the bathroom. We're a mess," laughed Hank.

"Damn, Hank, we've been at it for two hours. Look at the time!"

"Would you like to stay the night, since it's late and we're both naked?"

"Only if you promise to fuck me in the morning, stud!"

"Oh, how you do sweet-talk me!"

With that, Hank and Shawn went to bed after showering and fell asleep in each other's arms. Hank wondered what he had done right to receive such a reward as the now naked, sleeping man that was in his bed.

LATER that week, after deciding that the cruise would be undoable for all four of the friends, Dean and Pat decided to go to the gay campground in the Greenbelt area. It was one of those all-gay-male campgrounds where a man could do pretty much anything his heart desired. Pat had asked Hank and Shawn if they were interested, and they said yes.

The campground had anything that you could want. You could camp with some friends and enjoy the campfire cooking hotdogs or you could go to the glory-hole trailers or the play trail, where much more "earthy" activities were conducted. The day before they were supposed to leave for the campgrounds, Dean and Pat had to do some shopping at the camping store. They would need a tent and sleeping bags at the very least. This wasn't going to be like their memorable trip to the Waldorf, that was for sure.

Dean was a bit hesitant about going camping, as he had never really pursued any outdoor activities involving the woods and nature. It was funny to hear him talk about the mosquitoes and being worried about snakes.

"What if I wake up and there's a snake in my sleeping bag?" worried Dean

"The only thing waking up in your sleeping bag that would resemble a snake will be my cock! It's really not that bad; you zip up your tent and sleeping bag and nothing can really get to you," Pat replied.

"Okay, you're the butch one. Anything to make you happy," Dean said with a smile.

They selected some fire-starting gear along with the tent and sleeping bags and walked up to the checkout lane.

"That will be two hundred and forty-seven fifty," said the clerk.

"At least it's not twenty-eight hundred like that cruise would have been," Pat said, as Dean flinched at the sticker shock.

Two sleeping bags, two flashlights, a pup tent and some fire-starting equipment were all they would need. The campground was only partially woods and nature, since the owners had set up a dancing area in a little pavilion where you could party at night. They also had a small outdoor café where you could purchase food if snacks and fire-roasted hotdogs weren't enough to keep you full. It really wouldn't be all that bad, and it would certainly be very different from what they were all used to doing over a weekend.

"I'm starting to get a little excited about going out into the woods with my man, getting all dirty and sweaty, just relaxing in a place where we can do whatever it is that our hearts desire," Dean said with an evil grin.

One of Pat's deepest fantasies involved having sex in a public place where someone could watch if they wanted to. He never knew how Dean would react if he were to tell him that so he never did. He could tell by the smile on Dean's face that he had a shot at it happening this weekend. This was the kind of place where people hoped spontaneous sex happened near the fire pit next to their campsite.

The other good thing about the campground was that they had a rule: no cameras or video recording equipment allowed past the front gate, and if you were caught with one in the campground you were immediately removed.

The two couples had very little to worry about this time if they let themselves get carried away.

"Dean, do you think we should just call off tomorrow and go to the campground a day early?"

"That sounds like a good idea; an extra day where we could be all Grizzly Adams," Dean replied.

"Okay. I'll call Hank and see what he thinks."

After they loaded the camping gear into the car he dialed Hank's phone number and waited for him to answer.

"Hey, Hank. How's it going?"

"Not bad. What's up?"

"Dean and I had an idea. How about we all call off work tomorrow and just go to the campground a day early? That way we aren't fumbling around late at night trying to set up tents and stuff," he asked Hank.

"Good idea. Shawn's off of work anyway and he only has one early class so I know he could do it without a problem," Hank responded.

"Great. Dean and I were going to hit a movie later. Do you want to come?"

"Shawn and I have plans tonight; sorry. So I'll just stay home and pound Shawn's ass," Hank said, half-jokingly.

"All right, guy. I'll see you tomorrow at ten o'clock," Pat said, hanging up.

D<small>EAN</small> and Pat drove home and prepared all of the camping gear. Dean went to the store and got beer and hotdogs and Pat got the cooler ready and everything else packed so they could just grab it when they were ready to go the next day.

This was going to be quite an adventure; Pat had heard some old friends were going to be at the campground as well, so he reserved the campsite next to theirs.

He was hoping this would be one weekend where they could cut loose and just party. The thought of forgetting work and all else while just being in the woods relaxing and playing with friends who wouldn't judge them sounded like heaven on earth.

The fun would all have to be within reason, of course, as there were still some boundaries he was unwilling to cross. Then again, there were some he just couldn't wait to hurdle over.

Later that night Dean and Pat went to the little theater that showed independent films, usually the artsy kind that Dean liked. Pat didn't hate the indy films; he just preferred more mainstream action movies.

"I don't like most of the gay films that are produced today. One of the main characters always dies of AIDS or something and there is almost never a happy ending," said Pat.

"Your favorite gay film has to be *Latter Days*. It was a great love story with a happy ending," said Dean.

"Let's grab some dinner. It'll be a while before we can eat in civilization again," he joked.

WHEN they got back home, they decided that they would pack the car then to save time the next day. That way they could sleep in and stay up all night partying with the boys at the campground.

They loaded the gear into the trunk and went inside.

"Okay, survivor, now we're all set for our tryst in the woods. So are we going to sit around the campfire and tell ghost stories as we roast marshmallows?" Dean jokingly asked.

"Naw, I was thinking more along the lines of taking you to the playground and pounding that tight little ass of yours on the swings. Then we can tell ghost stories and roast marshmallows," he replied, winking.

"Wanna get some practice?" asked Dean.

"Yeah, but first I better call into the desk sergeant and inform him I won't be on shift tomorrow."

The desk sergeant was surprised to get another call.

"Must be some kind of bug going around on your shift; you're the second one in ten minutes to call off from your platoon. Whatever it is, don't bring it in here," joked the faceless sergeant.

"Don't worry about that, Sarge, I'm sure I'll be feeling much better in a couple days."

The next morning everyone left for the campground.

"All set, Dean. Hank is going to meet us in the parking lot near the front gate. He's got some of his old army gear for camping. He told me to leave our tent at home as he has a tent that will fit all four of us very comfortably," Pat said. "Lock the door and let's get going. It's forty-five minutes to the campground and I'm sure that when we arrive, we will find Shawn and Hank waiting anxiously by the check-in building."

"Hi, guys. Nice to see you again. I've never been to a place like this before. This is going to be awesome," said Shawn.

Hank was dressed in cutoff shorts and a military-style army hat.

The clerk at the front desk was an older man who identified himself as the co-owner of the campground. After asking everyone for their ID, he gave them little blue membership cards that allowed them free admission the rest of the year and informed them that the volleyball courts and the pool would be open for the weekend.

"Oh boy, we are really roughing it. What time are the massages and pedicures?" joked Hank.

"Okay, then, soldier boy, if I were you, I wouldn't roam too far into the woods though. Some big bear might just grab your tight butt and take it for a ride," the man behind the desk said, smiling as he checked out Hank's ass.

Hank almost tripped running out of the check-in building in mock terror as they all laughed and went back to the cars to drive to the campsite.

It was a big, beautiful campground; it had to be at least three miles from the nearest highway. They entered the large wooden privacy fence and drove slowly down the dirt road, going over a wooden bridge that was near a waterfall. Beyond the waterfall was a rather large lake that looked like a vacation postcard.

"This is absolutely beautiful! I've never seen a waterfall that big," gasped Shawn.

"This is why I love to come out here. Nature, boys, and beers. What else could you want?" Pat asked with a grin.

They pulled up to their campsite and found that their friends Greg and Brian had already set up their little site and had a roaring fire going.

"Hey, Pat! Long time no see, you big studly cop you," said Greg. "Come here and let me give you a great big hug!"

He saw Dean stare at Greg like a lion that was ready to pounce.

Greg and Pat kissed each other on the cheek and then disengaged from the friendly embrace and helped everyone unload the equipment from the trunk. It would take more than just a few minutes to set up everything. Hank and Pat started work on the tent.

"Wow, Hank, this really is a big tent!"

"It's the kind we stayed in while we were in the desert, and I brought some air mattresses for us so we aren't sleeping on the ground," replied Hank.

"Cool, man. I'm not gonna ask how you got this stuff," Pat said, winking.

At that Hank just smiled and pounded the military-issued tent stakes into the ground with an olive-colored hammer as Shawn walked up behind Hank and simulated pounding Hank's ass.

"You wish! We both know who the pitcher and who the catcher is in this here love affair," Hank said, sticking his tongue out at Shawn.

"Keep this up and we're gonna end up at the playground a lot earlier than I thought; I also stole a pair of your handcuffs just for this occasion," Shawn said, as he gave Hank an evil look.

*****

"So, what are you boys going to do first? Volleyball, the pool, or maybe a little trek through the woods?" asked Greg.

"Naw, we were thinking of just hanging around the fire pit and getting drunk until the party later tonight," replied Hank.

"Party? What party?" Shawn asked with interest.

"Shawn, didn't you know it's mating season weekend? That means everyone gets drunk and heads to the play trail in the woods to fuck. You're only allowed to come to the party in your underwear," replied Greg.

Brian and Greg knew where the line was regarding these two couples. Pat had made sure to explain the boundaries to them before reserving a campground site next to them. However, a little flirting and looking never hurt anyone.

This is going to be one hell of a weekend, thought Pat as he watched Dean open the cooler and crack open the first of many beers. Pat felt content as he stretched out on a chaise lounge and watched Hank start a fire.

The boys sat in a circle around the fire talking about their relationships and past conquests when Greg decided to tell a story that was one of Brian's more embarrassing tales.

"We were at a party in this huge house. I only knew the guy through friends. The house was amazing, with four floors, staff quarters, and a finished basement that could have easily been used as a bar. Brian had been drinking something called a purple motherfucker, which, by the way, I have no idea what's in it, but it is purple," said Greg, smiling as Brian started to blush and shot Greg the evil eye for telling this story for what was probably the tenth time.

"So, Brian passes out on the pool table because he's drunk as shit. He had way too much to drink and all of a sudden this muscle-bound stud walks up to him and starts to rub his crotch and Brian starts getting rock-hard. The man begins to remove Brian's clothes and at this point Brian starts to wake up but instead of resisting, Brian couldn't rip his clothes off fast enough."

"Oh, come on. You make me sound like such a whore when you tell this story, and it gets more sordid every time you tell it," interjected Brian.

"If the shoe fits, sweetie," winked Greg. "So, anyway Brian's all but naked with the exception of having to rip off his underwear and expose his hot little ass for that big guy to tap. Now picture a large crowd of people standing around and Brian's ass is in the air just waiting to get pounded. The guy unzips his pants, pulling out this huge chunk of meat, and is getting ready to pound Brian's hole and then it happens. Brian throws up all over the pool table. The muscle boy almost instantly went limp and started to dry-heave, and you knew it was all over then. The best part was Brian turns around and asks him if he was gonna fuck him or what."

Greg smiled as the group around the fire all started laughing hysterically; that is, all except for Brian, who was now as red as a fire truck from embarrassment.

"Just you wait, bitch. I got all kinds of dirt on you too," said Brian, as he chugged his beer and headed for another well-deserved one.

"Well, I can tell this is going to be an interesting weekend. You two have been dating for two years now and you guys are always a handful when the alcohol is flowing. You always have to see who can out-embarrass or out-fuck the other. It's like a little contest where you compete with each other to see who can get the most men willing to come back to the tent or into the pigpen and fuck. You're nothing if not entertaining," said Pat with a laugh.

Thankfully, the other two couples had healthy relationships. There was nothing wrong with a little exploration, but there would be no need for competition.

"What the hell is the pigpen?" asked Dean.

"It's a small open area behind the dance hall where all the boys do whatever to whoever while basically acting like pigs; hence the name the pigpen," Brian said, matter-of-factly.

"Oh, I have got to see this place," said Hank.

"Spectator or player?" asked Shawn.

"I've got the only ass I want sitting right here next to me, but I've never seen a live orgy before," said Hank, chuckling.

"It's an incredibly clear night. Just look at those stars! You know, it's almost three o'clock in the morning and we've been drinking all night. Right, Brian?"

"Yeah, I know, Greg. But hearing about everyone's past debauchery sure is fun! You wanna go to bed?"

"Sure, but we don't necessarily have to go to sleep, now do we?"

Brian reached over and squeezed Greg's dick, which was visible through his slightly tight gym shorts.

"You know you have to get fucked tonight before we go to sleep, right?"

"Oh? Who did you have in mind to fuck? Anyone I know?" asked Greg with an evil smile.

"You know who it's going to be. Now let's walk over to that picnic table by the tree."

Pat watched as Brian took Greg's hand and they walked in the moonlight over to where people had eaten dinner not that long ago. They began by kissing; the deep passionate kind of kissing that usually curls one's toes. As they kissed, their hands roamed each other's bodies, exploring familiar turf. Brian slowly lowered Greg's shorts. When both men were hard, Brian gently turned Greg around and bent him over the picnic table as he began to apply lube to his finger and his cock. As he worked the lube into Greg's ass, Greg began to moan slightly, fully enjoying the probing finger and anticipating what was to come next.

Brian spread Greg's ass cheeks and began to press the head of his cock into the opening of Greg's ass. This was the single sex act that made Greg and Brian feel as if they were one. They didn't fuck any other men, although blow jobs were allowed. Finally, Brian's cock slipped past the tight opening and slid up Greg's ass until his balls rested against Greg's waiting ass.

"Damn, honey, that feels so good. Fuck me slowly and then just bang the shit out of me!"

Brian was happy to comply with Greg's request and began to slowly pull out and push back in, until both bodies were rocking in unison. As Brian began to pick up the pace, Greg grabbed onto the table harder so as to not be pushed around on the rough surface. After all, he didn't want a splinter in his own pecker!

Both men were enjoying this outdoor fuck in the middle of the night, which was being captured by the moon. The thought that one of the neighbors might be watching the two copulate made it even more exciting.

"Okay, Brian. Now really give it to me. Come on, baby. Blow your wad up my ass!"

After another dozen thrusts, Brian moaned loudly and slammed his cock into his lover one final time as he came spurt after spurt, filling the end of the rubber that he had put on. Finally, after having expended the pent-up load, he collapsed onto Greg's back with a sigh of contentment. The sweat from their bodies mingling with each other, their breathing began to return to normal.

As his dick pulled out of Greg's ass, Brian said, "Okay, now your turn, sweets. How do you want to get off?"

Greg stood up and turned around and Brian could see the cum glistening on his lover's stomach.

"I think that part has been taken care of," he said while looking down at his stomach and smiling.

"Okay, let's get cleaned up and get to bed before the sun comes up and it's time for breakfast."

They put their arms around each other and walked toward their tent, totally fulfilled from what had been a terrific day. If only all of their days could be spent just like this one, life would be great. But then again, that wouldn't be reality, and this place wouldn't be special.

MOST of the men got up around nine in the morning. Hank had gotten up earlier than the rest to get the campfire going.

"Morning. Slept well, I trust?" Pat asked Hank.

"I don't think I've had that much beer in a while. I was out like a rock. You could have all taken turns on my ass and I wouldn't have known it."

"Oh, you would have felt that," chided Brian, who was emerging from his tent.

"Keep it up. I got extra handcuffs for the likes of you, buddy," Hank said, smiling.

"Don't threaten me with a good time," Greg said, as he stretched, exposing his chiseled chest and six-pack abs.

"I thought I heard a bear or something out here last night. There was all this growling and moaning. I thought of reaching for my gun, but then I fell asleep again," Pat said with a chuckle. Greg reached for a breakfast bar from the cooler.

"Whoa, I'm working on breakfast right here! I brought all the military mess gear so that we could eat normal food." Hank whipped out what appeared to be a grate of some sort with two metal spits shoved into the ground, along with a frying pan and a dozen eggs.

"Our little Boy Scout, always prepared. Next thing you know he'll be helping old men across the street to the pigpen like a good scout," said Dean.

Hank picked up a raw egg and threw it at Dean, barely missing him.

Everyone had a good laugh, and Hank continued to work on breakfast. No one could really explain it but there was a different flavor to the food cooked in the open air, maybe because it was cooked over an open wood fire. But everyone agreed: it was damn good.

"So what's on the agenda today, boys?" asked Shawn.

"Greg and I are off to the trails. We're gonna go play voyeur for a while. You guys are welcome to come if you like, or come too." Brian winked.

Dean hesitated, and said, "I'm not too sure about that."

"Dean and I are going to sit around the camp for a bit. We might join you later."

"Shawn and I will join you. We've gotta see this," said Hank.

Pat watched Shawn load up a small cooler with some beers, and smiled as Shawn secretly stashed some lube and condoms in the side pouch. Having picked up on this, he knew there would be a bit more than just watching happening on that little expedition. The men took off, leaving Pat and Dean alone.

"Now that we are alone, will you tell me what's wrong, Dean?"

"This is all pretty new to me," Dean said. "I mean, I was no virgin when you met me, that's for sure, but most of my experiences were meeting people online or in bars. Going into the woods and watching guys fuck, or getting fucked while people watch, is kind of a quantum leap from that," he continued.

"Dean, if you're not comfortable with that, we can just sit here or go to the pool or something. There's a volleyball court near the pool, and I'm sure there will be lots of shirtless boys to play ball with."

"Sounds like a plan," Dean said, smiling and obviously very relieved.

As Dean and Pat headed down the hill to the pool area, they found naked studs lying all around on the lounge chairs, sunning themselves from top to bottom. The campground didn't allow sexual activity around the pool area for sanitation reasons, but you could be naked as a jaybird and stare until your eyes fell out of your head if you liked.

They found a set of chairs near the volleyball court and settled in. Dean opened the cooler and pulled out two bottles of Corona and they both started to drink, when a man who could have been the model for the statue of David walked by with at least an eleven-inch piece of meat hanging down for all the world to see. Dean nearly choked on his beer and it dribbled all down his chest and onto the ground.

The man knew exactly what he was doing and stopped right in front of the guys and purposely asked for directions to the play trail, pointing in different directions so that his hammer of Thor swung inches from their faces.

"You should ask that guy to see his permit for that thing. It has got to be a deadly weapon," Dean said to Pat, his mouth agape.

"That reminds me, Dean. I need to borrow a hammer to make sure the stakes are firmly in the ground at our tent. I think I'm gonna take a dip in the pool," he said. "I hope the cold water will help reduce this throbbing hard-on problem I've got."

After a short swim he emerged from the pool and walked toward Dean, dripping wet and smiling.

He could tell Dean was becoming more relaxed in this environment. It was either the immersion into this new world far from the sedate banks that Dean was used to, or the alcohol.

"Hey, it looks like the boys are putting together a volleyball game. Wanna play, Dean?"

"Sure. Let's get dirty and sweaty," Dean said with an uncharacteristic spurt of kink.

As they approached the volleyball court, he heard the organizer say, "All right, it's skins and shorts."

"Don't you mean skins and shirts?" asked Dean.

"Mary, you heard me. And just for that, you're on the skins team, so lose the shorts," said the man, with a slightly evil grin. Dean quickly removed his shorts. "Damn, boy, we sure know what team you're playing for," the organizer said.

"Well, look who it is, and just in time to play!" said Pat.

"You guys got room for Shawn and me?" asked Hank.

"Yeah, sure. You're on skins with us. Shawn's ass will distract them enough to let us win," observed Dean.

Shawn undid his shorts and bent over toward the opposing team as he removed them.

Pat watched as everyone playing volleyball decided they would be playing skins after just a few minutes. Though some of the guys playing should have just kept their shorts on, and lessened the eye pollution. Pat smiled and realized it was all in fun and kinda humorous, watching some of the guys hurt themselves when their big floppy balls hit against their bodies.

The game was basically four against four; it was a beautiful day for such a game. The sun was out and it had to be at least eighty degrees with a cool breeze. The boys were going all out, diving and jumping, letting their cocks flop in the wind.

Dean's inhibitions seemed to be totally gone by the end of the game. He walked up behind Pat with a raging hard-on, gave him a sweaty sand-covered hug, and sucked on his neck.

"Let's go shower off near the pool. I got sand in my ass crack and that doesn't feel as good as you'd think," he said with a laugh. "After all, it's a community shower and we can watch the boys soap up and wash each other's backs!"

After they all finished showering and put their shorts back on they decided they would return to the campsite and get some money to eat at the little café that was on the campground.

"That was some game," Pat said.

"Unbelievable, though I will say that is the last time I play shortsless," said Shawn.

"Why's that, Shawn?" asked Hank

"I'm going to be picking sand out of my ass for a month," he replied.

"All that diving and spiking; I'm beat. It was fun until that one guy showed up and thought he was on some beach in California playing professional volleyball. That guy was an ass," said Dean.

"Yeah, but it was still fun. All that naked flesh running around, not to mention the shower afterwards," Pat said as he slapped Dean on the ass.

It was nice to get away from work and be with friends for the weekend. The day was beautiful, the weather was perfect and the camaraderie was totally enjoyable. There was almost no other activity that he could think of that would so tightly cement his friendship with Hank.

The boys arrived at the campground and they all went into the tent and changed. Shawn had brought his little digital camera and decided that a group photo of the three couples would be nice. He knew cameras were forbidden so he was quick and careful.

After everyone was dressed they all lined up in front of the fire pit and the timer was set so that everyone would be included: Dean, Pat, Hank, Shawn, Greg, and Brian, smiling and with their arms around one another.

Dean then filled Greg and Brian in on the details of the volleyball game. The guys said they wished they could have been there to see Shawn dive for the ball naked, but they had been hiking all day in the nature area. No one needed a translator to figure out that the boys had been out planting their seed all over the forest.

There were no judgments to be made here; this was the place and time to be yourself. No one held anything against anyone else as long as long as people were honest with who and what they were. There was no need to put up some facade and pretend with these guys. That's what

Pat loved about the group of friends that he had and that was why he made sure that they were included in the camping trip.

The group arrived at the little outdoor café, which was nothing more than a grill-type kitchen in the registration building. It had a covered room and patio over a meandering stream with a beautiful view of the forest and the pool. The food was excellent, the kind that visitors had to eat at least once or they would feel the trip was incomplete.

Dean and Pat sat at the corner table with Hank and Shawn while Greg and Brian were flirting with another couple on the other side of the patio.

"Those two are like rabbits," said Shawn.

"Yeah, really. I've never seen anyone so horny," replied Hank.

"Jealous?"

Hank looked at him. "Of what? Having sex with everything that moves? I'm more of a one-man type of guy."

"So am I, but are you trying to tell me that you never experimented?" Shawn asked with genuine interest.

"I'm not sure that I want to get into this at the moment. After all, I'm with my new boyfriend."

"I've done a threesome or two," Shawn interjected.

Pat laughed as Dean nearly choked on his soda from the way Shawn had said that so casually.

"Oh, stop. Like you've never?" Shawn said dismissively. "I don't think that's a halo on your head, Dean, sweetie. I bet it's more of a cock ring," he continued.

The group had a good laugh at that comment.

Dean looked at Shawn, sizing him up, as he tried not to sound like a prude.

"Well, I didn't come out until recently so my innocence is still intact, unlike some people's."

Hank cleared his throat and coughed out the name "Pat."

"I'm not saying I wouldn't try anything new but I would never cheat on Pat either," said Dean with a wink to Pat.

"New stuff? Like what?" asked Shawn.

"Wouldn't you like to know?" replied Dean.

"Yes, enlighten me. What kind of new stuff?" he asked.

"Waiter, check, please," said Dean jokingly, as he snapped his fingers at a nonexistent waiter.

"Ha, ha, coward!" laughed Hank.

"Looks like you got some training to do, Mr. Pat," said Shawn.

"Oh, you guys are a riot and a handful. You're going to corrupt my innocent Dean," he said, as he kissed Dean on the lips, trying to help him escape what was obviously becoming an uncomfortable conversation.

Pat was quite interested in what Dean meant by new stuff, though. Was Dean going to help him fulfill his public sex fantasy or was Dean going a little more toward the darker side?

He sure hoped not. He didn't just want vanilla sex but he didn't want to make the Marquis de Sade look like an amateur either.

The guys met back up with Brian and Greg and found that they had gotten everyone in the group invited to a site party later on in the day. It was at a nudist colony that was within the camp. The camp was clothing-optional but the nudist rule was no clothing allowed, and for the most part they didn't care, as they had all been naked for the volleyball game and this would be no different. By this time, everyone knew what everyone else was packing in their shorts anyway.

They all gathered at the campsite and decided to sit around for a bit and relax; it had been a fun-filled day and they were all drained from the alcohol, volleyball, and the interesting conversation at lunch.

As the boys settled around the fire pit and grabbed bottles of water to rehydrate, they all heard a loud crack and a man loudly groan. Shawn and Dean jumped up and looked around, and Greg and Brian just sat there staring at something behind them. The campsite next to the boys consisted of eight men dressed in leather ass-less chaps, and they were paddling one another.

The boys formed a semicircle around the fire pit and decided to watch the show. Hell, if they wanted it to be private they wouldn't be doing it outside.

The leather-clad boys had one man dressed like the gimp from *Pulp Fiction* and it seemed he was taking the brunt of the abuse, but absolutely loving it. He was calling whoever was paddling him "master" and was begging for forgiveness for being a bad boy all day.

Dean's eyes were glued to the spectacle; it was as if he had just seen the mother ship land and all the aliens had gotten out to ask for directions to the nearest gay bar.

The men continued to punish their boy and then took turns fucking him; it was truly the raunchiest thing Dean had seen in his life. The man had to have taken at least seven dicks after getting his ass beaten.

Shawn looked at the rest of the men after the spectacle had ended and said, "That was so dirty I think that I need another shower just to feel clean again. I don't have anything against the whole S&M scene or leather; I'm just not into it for myself."

Greg and Brian started to pack up some beer in a portable cooler for the walk to the nudist colony.

"Are we ready to go?" asked Brian.

"Yeah. This should be interesting," said Hank.

"It's not going to be like what we just watched, is it? I don't think I could handle any more of that," Dean stated in a shaky voice.

"Wuss," said Greg.

They all had a laugh; the little leather show was something that even Pat hadn't seen in his experimental stage of exploring his sexuality.

"Oh, come on, Dean. The nudist colony is just like the rest of the campground! I'm not saying sex won't happen or that it will. It's just another place to go and another party with free booze and food, so let's get rolling," Brian said, as he gulped the last of his water from the bottle.

Everyone got up and they started their walk through the woods. The path was a well-kept dirt trail cutting through the forest. Along the way people had trailers set up where they would rent a spot for the entire year and live there during the summer months. Pat could only imagine how nice it must be to live in a place where everyone is gay and do whatever you want without any worries about who would find out or what your neighbors thought.

The group arrived at the tall wooden fence that separated the nudist colony from the rest of the camp. There was a large sign above what looked like several coat hooks. It read: *Leave your clothing, your judgments and your inhibitions behind. Before you open the gate, open your mind.*

They all stripped down and placed their clothes in a backpack that Hank had brought with him. They didn't want to have their clothing stolen by some jokester or thief and then have to walk back to the campground naked, even though some of the dirtier boys in the place might have loved that – six hot naked studs parading around, cocks in the wind.

Greg and Brian walked off in their own direction. They seemed to have been here before and knew several of the other guys who were standing buck-ass naked near the buffet table.

"Those boys are like the mayors of Gaytown," said Dean.

"How do you think I met them, Dean? They came over to me and chatted me up. They don't care what anyone thinks or says, and that is what makes me like them so much," he said.

"Did you ever have sex with them?" asked Dean.

"What does that matter? I don't cheat on you and I never would; you're the man I want to spend the rest of my life with," he said.

"That would be a yes, I take it," said Dean, with a glare. Dean had some experiences of his own before he met Pat, though the more alcohol he drank and the more sex he saw at the campground made him wonder what else he might have missed out on by playing the part of a goody two-shoes in his sex life.

"Are you jealous?"

"A little."

"Well, don't be. Meaningless, mechanical sex with someone you don't care about is nothing compared to nailing the one you love," he said as he fondled Dean's cock and kissed him deeply.

Pat noticed that half of the nudist colony stopped what they were doing in order to watch Dean and Pat make out. He knew that both of them were rock-hard at the moment and that everyone was hoping to watch the show.

Before Dean and Pat knew it they were the center of attention. Dean became a little self-conscious and stopped kissing Pat and tried to hide his hard-on.

"Good luck hiding that piece of meat, honey!" someone from the crowd shouted.

"I got somewhere you can hide that thing!" yelled someone else.

The crowd all laughed and Dean relaxed a little bit. Dean realized everyone was hard after that show and that everyone was also naked; not to mention he was sporting one of the more lethal weapons at this party.

Hank came over to them and said, "Look at you two. Here five seconds and you're at it already. Keep this up and I'm gonna start carrying ice water around with me to douse you two."

"How hot, publicly making out while rubbing each other's cocks in front of fifty naked men," Shawn said.

With that, Hank grabbed Shawn by the shoulders and pushed him face-first against the wall, pushing his cock against Shawn's smooth ass.

"Mmmmm, warm," said Hank.

Hank started to suck on Shawn's neck and shoulders and all Shawn could do was moan in pleasure. He was hard as a rock and leaking precum. Hank grabbed Shawn by his short military-style hair and pulled Shawn's head back a little and whispered in his ear, "I'd love nothing more than to fuck that little hole of yours right here and now; I'd love to let fifty people watch me do it."

Hank began pushing his way inside of Shawn. Shawn bent over slightly to show his submission since he wanted to show Hank that he wanted it too. This was all Hank really wanted at that moment: for Shawn to show public submission to him. Both men got off mentally letting everyone know which roles they played in their newborn relationship. Hank had entered Shawn's ass about an inch, and instead of shoving it all the way in, he pulled out until Shawn's ass was free from the intruding member.

"It's okay, Hank. Fuck me if you want to. I can take it like this."

"Nah, I want to fuck you more in private, baby. You showed that your ass is mine anytime I want it, and I like that. Tonight, I take it all, babe."

"You're the boss," Shawn said, with a smile that could melt steel.

Then it happened. Someone shouted, "Hey, put that fucking camera away now!"

One of the campers hadn't been able to resist trying to sneak a video of the two hot studs fucking. The founders of the nudist colony quickly escorted the man with the camera out of the camp and confiscated the videotape.

Hank and Shawn quickly stopped what they were doing. It had been hot, but the camera thing had kind of spooked Hank, a flashback of the drug dealer episode that halted what he was doing altogether.

Pat walked over to the man being escorted out of the campground, looked him square in the eye and said, "What the fuck is wrong with you? This is the one place where we can be ourselves and some dickhead like you has to ruin it because you can't follow the simple rules. Go buy some fucking porn and jerk off to that, you douche bag! If I didn't have the job I did on the outside I would punch you in the face and break your nose!" he screamed.

Pat was surprised at how angry he was at what had just transpired.

Dean walked up to the man and said, "Thank god I don't have to worry about that," shoving the guy out the front wooden gate and slamming it behind him.

"Asshole!" shouted Shawn.

"Damn, that was hot, but I wasn't gonna do it anyway," said Hank.

"We'll pick up where we left off later, stud," said Shawn.

The rest of the party was pretty unremarkable. A few guys making out, some guys blowing each other and then just the regular guys who just liked to be naked who were standing around talking.

It was kind of strange; like being in some alternate universe. These men were buck naked, wearing nothing but a beer can and a smile, and they were talking like they were in a restaurant or a coffeehouse. Some discussed work and relationships and others discussed business deals. It was a great place to spend a Saturday afternoon with friends.

"Damn, Hank, I've never seen you so sexually aggressive before," Pat said. "I didn't expect that!"

"I don't know what came over me. Shawn egged me on and bam, it almost went down like that. You don't feel weird because you saw me like that, do you?" asked Hank.

"No way, dude. It was kind of a turn-on. Not because I want to fuck you or anything. It's just the whole situation was so damn erotic," he said in a whispered voice.

"Besides, that's why we are here. Now we can expose our true selves," said Hank, looking down at Pat's package and ass in mock interest.

Pat couldn't help but laugh. "Oh stop, you're making me blush."

"Well, it looks like everyone has had their fill of the nudist colony and it's almost time for dinner, so why don't we all head back to the campsite?" suggested Greg.

"Yeah, I brought some nice steaks for us to cook over the fire. They were frozen but they should be thawed out in the cooler by now," said Shawn.

"Mmmmm, big chunks of meat for dinner. Sounds hot," said Brian, in a mock sultry voice.

"I think you've had enough meat for now," said Greg, as he winked at his partner.

They had quite an open relationship and they didn't care who knew it.

Hank set up the fire pit for grilling steaks. He took out two metal spikes and put a grilling grate on top. The smell of the barbequing meat was amazing and motivated Greg and Brian to make the salad. You could tell that these two had been at the campground before as they had come prepared with all the needed tools to cut up the vegetables, along with all of the vegetables and dressing.

Later they all sat on folding chairs near the smoldering fire pit, enjoying the feeling of full bellies and the relief from the mosquitoes that being near a smoky fire brought them.

"So what's tonight's agenda, boys?" asked Shawn to no one in particular.

"The dance pavilion, and some of the more adventurous guys may go into the pigpen," said Greg.

"Hey, I've heard of the pigpen but have never been there," said Dean, smiling.

"Nothing wrong with it, if that's your thing. I like to watch and be watched," said Shawn.

"Yeah, we saw that, sweetie," said Brian smiling.

"Oh, lord, I hope what happens in Vegas stays in Vegas," said Hank.

"Yes, yes, we know. Don't talk outside of church," said Greg.

"Well, why don't we get cleaned up and get ready for a night of partying?" Dean asked.

Some of the guys took showers, while others changed clothes and put on cologne and bug repellant, which made for a rather odd smell. When everyone was ready, they left for the pavilion.

As the boys approached the dance hall, the music of Erasure's latest album beat through the air, filling the guys with the gyrating vibrations of dance. It was all they needed, combined with the sexual tension of the day, to hit the hall, like Jesse James hitting a bank.

As they walked through the front door, Pat grabbed Dean and off onto the dance floor they went. Their bodies began to keep time with the beat of the music, making their tight white T-shirts hug their ample chests even more. This only served to complement their choice of tight 501s and work boots for the rest of the gear for the dance.

Hank and Shawn watched in utter amazement at how good Pat and Dean looked on the dance floor. It was obvious that both had done some dancing in the days before this little camping trip. The pair even drew the admiring glances of the others in the pavilion, drawn by the withering, pulsating bodies of the two sexy, and obviously in love, men.

"Well fuck this, they ain't gonna steal the show, babe. Let's hit the floor and show them what we got!" Shawn yelled as he grabbed Hank's hand and moved onto the floor next to Pat and Dean.

As another song came on from the same group, the beat never let up from the previous song, and the mood was kept through the changeover. Now instead of just two hunks on the floor moving like poetry in motion, there were four men to stare at and admire. In fact, the rest of the dancers moved away slightly, giving the foursome their own center of attention in the middle of the crowded room.

None of them ever noticed as they were consumed by the beat of the music and the beers previously consumed at the campsite. As the temperature went up in the room, the shirts began to come off. The first one to show skin was Pat and that was all it took. Before long, everyone had their shirts off, showing bodies in all degrees of shape and size. An atmosphere of brotherly camaraderie was created in the middle of nowhere on a dance floor that no one but the guests could see.

As the music played on, the intensity of the dancing combined with the pulsating colors increased to the point that the entire room was swaying to the music in a climactic orgy of sexuality and celebration. This was what it was like to be a gay man! Nothing could make it clearer or more understandable in this sea of single purpose. Everyone was there to have a good time, dance, drink, fuck, and celebrate life. All the guys present had to deal with the harshness of life on a daily basis outside the walls of the campgrounds, but not here. This moment in time was a celebration of pure joy in whom and what everyone had been destined to become. Life could be good, even if it was only temporary!

During a break from dancing, a round of beer was ordered, and they became busy wiping the sweat off their faces and chests with their T-shirts. As Hank looked around at everyone, he noticed that without exception everyone was smiling and having a great time.

"This was a great idea, Pat. Thanks from coming up with it and inviting us to experience the freedom this place gives us. We gotta come back here again this summer at least one more time," Hank said.

"Hank, how could I come up here and not invite the guy who has become my best friend, not to mention his new college stud boyfriend!"

Hank smiled at the comment. He liked that Pat thought of him as his "best friend."

"Yeah, well, just remember that the stud boyfriend is taken. I see how you look at him, my friend," Hank said loud enough so that Dean and Shawn could hear. They all laughed.

Pat wasn't feeling any pain. He looked over at Shawn and nodded approvingly.

"You did all right, my friend. He is a keeper."

"I wanna go back to the pigpen and see what there is to see!" Shawn practically squealed.

Once again, everyone laughed, and they moved to the door to go out back. As they took their places along a railing to look down to the play area, Greg and Brian joined them in their voyeurism.

Everyone watched for a moment in complete silence. Dean's jaw dropped open. There in the pen were about thirteen men getting buttfucked in various positions with a lot of grunting and moaning going on. Additionally, blowjobs were being given against trees and a fake glory-hole had been setup. Some of the men were hot, while others had seen better days. All of the men were lost in the sexuality of the moment, and having an audience only added to their enjoyment.

As they watched, Pat noticed that Hank had reached over and was fondling Shawn's basket. Shawn reacted with an impressive swelling in his tight jeans. At the sight of this and all of the sex going on around him, he began to get very horny and knew that before the sun came up, he would be cumming in Dean. The thought of fucking in the tent, lying next to his buddies was an incredible turn-on. What if Hank and Shawn were fucking too? *Damn,* he thought, *I wouldn't mind seeing that either.* Before he realized it, he too was showing a nice bulge in his jeans. He moved Dean's hand over to his basket and pressed it into the lump.

Dean turned toward him and kissed him right then and there. It was a long, deep, and passionate kiss with lots of tongue. The conservative banker was now kissing a man and groping his ass in public in front of dozens of men, and he could care less. By the time the kiss finished, Dean was also showing a hard-on.

As the beat of a new song washed over them through the night air, they decided to return to the dance floor for one more dance before heading back to the campsite. As they burst through the doors and took to the floor, the crowd parted once again, giving them their space. Everyone had heard there were cops in the camp as guests, and they had figured out that those cops were Pat and Hank. This only added to the two couples' allure. It didn't take long for the music to work its magic as they began to get lost once more in the beat of the music and the movement of the bodies around them. The only difference now was that the four of them looked into the eyes of their partners communicating that thing that does not need to be said out loud: "I love you and want your sex."

As if it were a sign, "Sunday Girl," the same Erasure song that had begun their night, began to play. They all laughed at this coincidence. They danced until the end of the song and finally filed out of the dance hall, tired but happy, as the last notes of the song began to fade in their memories. Each of them held hands as they trekked back to the campsite, all silently smiling in the night air as they thought about the pleasure and release that was pending for each man. Pat couldn't be more pleased with the way the night had gone so far.

When they arrived, they soon learned that Brian and Greg had beaten them back to the campsite. They were already in their tent, and apparently in flagrante delicto.

"And I thought you were fast, Hank," observed Shawn with a laugh.

"Well, the fire is almost out and it's late. Shall we hit the sleeping bags?" Pat asked.

"Sure. You two want to go first so you can change in privacy?" asked Shawn.

"Nah, not necessary. We're all friends here," Pat replied.

"Yeah, you just want to see Shawn out of his jeans again!" accused Hank with a wink.

"Then let's give Pat what he wants, darling. He is your best friend, after all," Shawn said.

Everyone chuckled and headed into the tent, which was just big enough for four adults. While it was a little tight, everyone was able to climb out of their clothes and get into their sleeping bags or on an air mattress.

As they all lay there for a moment, the moans and grunts from Brian's tent wafted over into their tent. Shawn was the first to start snickering, which set off everyone else. Before long, all four of them were laying in their tent laughing at the lovemaking noises from their neighbors.

"For God's sake, Brian, you two sound like heifers in heat. Keep it down over there!" yelled Hank.

"Oh, fuck you, you're just jealous that you're not getting laid; now shut the fuck up!" came the response from Brian.

Once again, everyone broke out laughing at the indignant response from their friend.

"Well, let's do something about that 'getting laid' thing, shall we?" asked Shawn of Hank.

"Okay, you don't have to ask me twice, but let's keep the noise down so we don't get made fun of by the entire camp, let alone Brian and Greg, or these two," Hank said, while motioning toward Dean and Pat.

The sound of the zipper coming down on two sleeping bags filled the tent as Shawn and Hank opened up their sleeping bags. Shawn initially took the aggressive posture and kissed Hank while Hank was on his back, while groping Hank's cock and balls. Shawn was sexed up from the night's activities and it showed. Shawn moved his tongue down onto Hank's chest where he licked each nipple as he sucked on them, making them rigid. Hank couldn't help himself as he let out a little moan. Hank's nipples were two of the most sensitive spots on his body and Shawn knew it and he worked them.

Pat felt himself getting hard watching his two friends begin to make love. He reached over to Dean's crotch and was surprised to find Dean hard as a rock. *So, he is into watching those two get it on*, he thought to himself.

They could just barely make out what was happening because of the fading light of the campfire. Shawn moved his head down Hank's body until he had reached his cock, where he quickly took the shaft into his mouth and gently sucked.

He made just the faintest sucking noise, which was loud enough to let Dean and Pat know what was going on. Pat kicked his shorts off and then took Dean's underwear off so that they were both lying naked on their mattress. Dean surprised him by kicking off the sheet that had covered them and exposing their nakedness to Shawn and Hank. All pretense of not looking at their friends make love was now dispensed with as Pat leaned up on one elbow so that he could watch the unfolding action more comfortably. With his other hand, he began to play with Dean's engorged cock and balls. *Why the fuck not*, he thought to himself; they were hot looking-guys and they were friends sharing an intimate thing that friends could share if they so desired.

Hank turned his head and saw that his friends were very interested in what he and Shawn were doing. Hank also saw that both of his friends were erect and playing around with each other while watching Shawn give head. Hank almost blew his load just realizing the situation inside the tent.

He pulled Shawn's head off his cock and pushed him onto his back. He then took the aggressive stance and kissed Shawn and quickly moved to his pecs, which he licked and sucked as Shawn had done for him.

After watching Hank, Pat went down on Dean and didn't bother to hide the noise that was made by hungrily sucking his lover's cock, which made both Hank and Shawn stop and watch.

Motivated by what he saw, Hank went down on Shawn again and gagged as he tried to swallow all of Shawn without taking his time. Taking a deep breath, he backed off a little. Now both Hank and Pat were giving their lovers blow jobs that were slow and easy. Hank wanted the lovemaking to last more than a quick drunken blow job.

Dean pulled Pat's head off his cock as he began to get close and didn't want to spoil the experience by cumming too early. Hank took the opportunity to pull up off of Shawn's meaty cock as well. Hank and Pat both openly looked at the bodies of the other's lovers. Even in the fading light, enough details could be seen to make it a highly charged sexual atmosphere.

Dean and Shawn knew what was going on and neither made a move to end it before it began. Both Hank and Pat saw that as their nonverbal consent to a foursome if that's what they all wanted. It was obvious that all of them liked one another's bodies and the friendship that they shared. To Shawn, the most personal thing he could give to a friend was the pleasure of his body.

Pat made the first move and told himself he would stop dead in his tracks if he were reading the situation wrong. He reached over and took Shawn's cock in his hand and began to lightly jack it. He had read the situation correctly; there were no protests from Shawn, Hank, or Dean.

As he began to fondle Shawn, Hank moved around Pat and took Dean's weighty cock in his hands as well, effectively changing partners for the moment. Now both of them held their best friend's lover's cock in their hands as they looked down at the naked bodies of the other's mate. Hank then took the next step and ran his tongue over Dean's shaft and began to work on Dean's balls. Seeing this, Pat decided to get his taste of a cock he had wondered about since the first day he had met Shawn. He greedily sucked on Shawn's big dick, taking all but about two inches down his throat as he played with Shawn's balls. Shawn reached up and pulled Pat over him into a sixty-nine position so that he could suck his cock as well. It didn't take long before Hank followed suit and all four of them were sucking cock.

Because of the size of the tent, both Hank and Pat were on top of their temporary sexual partners while doing sixty-nine. This allowed Pat to drill his cock down into Shawn's hungry cock-sucking mouth as well as Hank to ram Dean's mouth.

Shawn pushed Pat's head off his cock, as he was getting close. Pat pulled his cock out of Shawn's mouth and moved off of Shawn's body. Since Hank had not stopped blowing Dean, he lightly tapped his friend on the head and said, "Time to give it a rest for a moment." As Dean and Hank separated, and they returned to their partners, he sighed heavily and said, "Damn, that was good. Thanks, you guys, for letting that happen."

"Okay, I want to see you go down on Hank now, Pat," Shawn said with a smile.

"Ahh, no. That would be too weird, I think. Hank is a hot guy and all, but we work together and I don't think we want to mix dick with the job. Right, Hank?"

"Nope, I agree. Getting to know our partners is one thing, but Pat and I have a special bond that does not include doing each other."

"Booo," said Shawn, "I wanted to see two cops blow each other!"

Pat reached over and grabbed Hank's dick and said, "That's as much as you will ever see."

Hank agreed and returned the favor.

"As for you, my love, get your legs over my shoulders," Pat said to Dean.

Dean did not hesitate to comply with his order. As Pat lifted his legs over his shoulders, he pulled Dean up even further so that his ass was elevated to the point that he could perform what was done only occasionally: he ate his lover's ass out while Hank and Shawn watched, their cocks once again becoming rigid.

"Ahh, fuck, Pat. That's good; don't stop!"

His mumbled response was, "Yes, dear."

"Hey, I want some of that too!" whispered Shawn to Hank.

"No problem, stud. Lift those legs to heaven!"

Now both of the guys were eating out their lovers' asses getting them ready for what they both knew they would be doing shortly. Both Hank and Pat loved nothing better than fucking a tight ass that appreciated the service. As both men on the receiving end of the tongues began to moan loudly, one word pierced the night air:

"Pigs!"

Everyone laughed out loud before returning to the pleasure they were enjoying.

"I guess that was Brian's payback editorial comment on the situation in return for the harassment we gave them earlier in the night," said Dean with a snicker.

After a few more minutes of ecstasy, Dean had enough and pleaded with his lover.

"Holy fuck, Pat! Will you shove your cock up my ass now?"

"You bet, lover boy. I'm all about 'to serve and protect'."

He reached into the bag and drew out a rubber and lube and began to apply both to his cock. He then placed a generous amount of lube into Dean's waiting ass. Even the feeling of his finger entering his orifice was enough for Dean to see stars.

Dean moved up and adjusted his ass so that it was at the right level for Pat to enter him. As he began to press into Dean's hole, Dean pushed against his cock to make it faster. He slipped past the initial resistance and entered into Dean's hot tight ass with an audible sigh.

"Oh fuck, that feels great," Pat said, as he let his cock sit for a moment so that Dean's ass would fully adjust and he could commence pounding his ass.

Hank followed suit and lubed up Shawn and quickly entered his lover's ass. Now both of them began to slowly fuck their boyfriends.

Time became suspended for all four men as they enjoyed the sheer intimacy and raw sexuality that was involved in fucking another man. Both Shawn and Dean began to moan once again, revealing how much they were into the action that was taking place. Hank and Pat began to fuck in unison without even realizing it. Both of them worked on the in-stroke together as they picked up the speed of their thrusts.

As the fucking picked up in intensity, they began to moan also, so that all four of them were now moaning and whispering commands of encouragement to one another.

"Come on, Hank. Fuck me hard, and give it to me like you wanted to do at the pool today. Fuck me; fuck me like you mean it!"

Both men were now slam-fucking their boyfriends in an orgy of excitement and pure sexuality. Hank moaned that special moan that signaled he was going to explode at any moment.

"Oh, fuck!"

"Come on, babe, give me your load," urged Shawn.

When Pat heard Hank cumming, he too began to explode into Dean's muscular ass.

"Dean, I'm cumming too, ahhhhhh."

Both men erupted in violent spasms of spurting cum as they rocked in and out of their boyfriends' asses. Only when the last drop had been ejaculated did each man collapse on top of his lover, spent and satisfied.

As their cocks began to ease out of their lovers' asses, both men pulled off the rubbers that had been put into service and put them into a Kleenex.

"Now, for your cock, babe," said Pat.

"I'm fine, stud. I came about two minutes into the fucking you gave me," Dean said with a smile.

He ran his hand over Dean's chest and felt the warm stickiness that signaled the presence of ejaculate.

"You damn sure did," he said with a snicker. "Good boy."

"Well, *I* still want my dick sucked. Now get down on it, mister," Shawn ordered Hank.

"With pleasure, my love."

Dean and Pat watched as Hank gobbled up Shawn's waiting phallus, slowly sucking the entire shaft as Shawn withered in pure pleasure. It didn't take long before Shawn began to buck wildly as he shot stream after stream of hot cum into the waiting mouth and throat of his lover.

Finally, Shawn's arched back went flat onto the floor of the tent, signaling an end to the climax. A look of peace descended upon his face in the dim firelight. His cock flopped out of Hank's mouth and made a loud noise as it hit his stomach.

Hank collapsed on top of Shawn in utter contentment as both men had enjoyed what was an earth-moving climax. In fact, peace descended upon the entire tent even though Pat had grown hard again at the site of his best friend sucking off his boyfriend.

Dean felt the hard-on pressing into his side and he turned to Pat and said, "Forget about it. It's time for sleep, horn dog!"

"Okay, I won't press my luck. Goodnight, stud, and to you two as well!" he said.

THE next morning, everyone woke to the sound of breakfast being cooked at the fire pit and the idle chatter between Brian and Greg. From the sound of their hushed tones, both guys were slightly hung over.

As they crawled out of their tent and into the morning sunlight, the rest of the men got up and stretched and yawned.

"Good morning, sunshine," said Greg pleasantly.

"Good morning, guys," replied all four of them.

"I'd say by the level of noise coming out of your tent last night, that you four had quite the party in there, or would I be wrong?" asked Brian with a leer.

Hank chose to respond to the statement by saying, "As far as I'm concerned, a good time was had by all, thank you very much."

"Indeed," Greg observed with a smile.

"Yeah, well all I know is that I have a sore ass this morning," chided Shawn.

"Hey, I can't help it that I'm such a stud, and you have such a pliable ass, now can I?" asked Hank.

All four of them broke out in wide smiles, confirming that a party did occur and was enjoyed by all of them. Brian and Greg obviously wished that they had been included in the little orgy that took place in the tent beside them. Envy dripped off of both their faces.

It was almost eleven by the time they were done with breakfast. They decided it was time to pack up and leave this little piece of paradise and return to the real world. As they were driving through the gate, all four of them looked over their shoulders and commented that they definitely would be back. That was just too much fun!

Chapter Eight
"You Didn't Just Say That!"

UPON his return to work, Pat's first shift back had been pretty uneventful, considering all that had been happening in the past few weeks. As a cop, he should know better than to ever utter or even think anything that sounds like, "I'm bored" or "It's slow tonight." Those two phrases seemed to invoke some sort of dark unseen force that almost immediately causes all hell to break loose.

Pat decided he would stop at the 7-Eleven and say hello to Shawn. He and Capstone had been dating for more than a few weeks now and he could tell Hank was very happy.

The fact that he hadn't had any coffee all night was getting more evident throughout the shift. On more than one occasion during the night, he caught himself almost falling asleep; his eyes would begin to close and his head would drop. He decided he definitely needed some caffeine.

The 7-Eleven was as empty as it always was around this time, save for one of the increasingly regular customers. In the parking lot was Capstone's police cruiser; he had beaten Pat to the store and was already having coffee and conversing with Shawn.

As he pulled into the parking lot he could see Capstone giving him a wave hello, as did Shawn. They were both smiling and you could tell just by looking at them how attracted to each other they were, not to mention the fact that they were in the throes of young love. It seemed it wasn't all that long ago that he went through the same thing with Dean.

He walked in and sarcastically said, "Aww, look at the happy couple. When are you two going to start having kids and make me an uncle?"

Shawn rolled his eyes and Capstone said, "Wouldn't you be called Aunt Pat?"

"I'll just ignore that attack on my masculinity, Capstone, but I won't forget it. Payback's a bitch!"

As he walked back to the coffee station to get his usual cup of coffee, he started to notice that since Capstone and Shawn had been dating the coffee was a little better than it used to be. It was nice to think that maybe Shawn was making better coffee because he was falling in love and now cared whether or not his man drank good stuff.

He walked up to the counter where Capstone was standing holding his coffee. Hank looked at Pat and said, "I don't want to jinx us, but man, it's quiet!"

Pat feigned annoyance and rolled his eyes.

"Great! You know what happens now, right? It's going to get crazy!" he said.

Shawn said with a smile, "With you two here, I'll never fulfill that hot robber fantasy I have. The one where he comes in and takes advantage of me. So get out there and serve and protect."

"Oh, really?" Capstone said, pretending to be jealous.

Shawn just winked and shot Capstone a smile.

"Well guys, since we just said things were slow, I guess I better get out there and get ready for the shit storm coming our way." Pat grabbed his coffee from the countertop near the register and headed out the door. Hank wasn't far behind him.

"You know, the last time we wanted action we got into that whole mess with the drug dealer," Pat said as he walked to his police car.

"How could I forget?" Capstone replied.

It had been a little more than six weeks since he'd had the chat with Lieutenant Farrell. Pat had erased the video from the chip using his cell phone. However, as promised, he kept the chip taped on the inside of his locker door as a reminder that someone was always watching. He had even bought a fish and named him "Poofter."

Lieutenant Farrell hadn't said much after that incident. Pat wasn't sure if he was uncomfortable with the fact that he and Capstone were gay or if he was just too busy to chat.

When he passed the Lieutenant in the hallway he would give him a cordial good morning but they never really had any conversation that resembled their last one.

Sergeant Durkin didn't seem to care much about the incident, other than what he said in his office that day. The whole issue was never again addressed. Pat guessed the police environment had evolved since the old days.

A lot of things had happened since the drug dealer had threatened to out Pat and Hank. For one thing, gay boys were still turning up murdered, and as of yet the department had no suspects.

There was something odd about the way the boys were drugged and strangled. The detectives assigned to the case had determined that this definitely was the killer's method of operation.

The motive and what the men had in common was still a mystery to the detectives. They were unable to find a common denominator, which made identifying a suspect even more difficult. One thing was noted, however: None of the victims' clothing included belts.

Pat had decided that he would sit in the parking lot of one of the many closed Starbucks coffeehouses in the area to monitor traffic as well as any suspicious activity. It was two in the morning and this seemed as good a place as any to sit and wait.

It was getting very boring, just sitting in a police car, hearing nothing but the usual mundane radio traffic going back and forth between dispatch and the many county police units, so he pushed the power button on the stereo and it came to life.

The station that was currently on had the voice of an annoying talk show host blabbing about the usual right-wing crap. The host reminded Pat of some right-wing religious whacko. He presented clumsy, ignorant, preconceived and misguided religious views, and went on and on about how independently he thought from the mainstream media, à la Bill O'Reilly.

Tonight he was on a rant about the governor and his policies regarding euthanasia. He claimed the governor's support for such a thing was sinfully wrong.

"Why doesn't he just support abortion and all other forms of murder while he's at it?" the commentator asked. "For God's sake, he's Republican! What's the party coming to?"

Pat quickly turned the radio off so that he didn't have to listen to the moron end up in his usual gay-bashing mode, which he considered part of the standard operating procedure for these right-wing nutcases.

As he continued monitoring what little traffic there was on the highway at this time of night, a white Chevy Corsica came speeding into view. It swerved into the oncoming lane of traffic. Fortunately there were no other cars on the road. The car continued past the cruiser at a high rate of speed.

Pat activated his emergency lights and sirens and radioed into dispatch.

"Adam 5. I'll be attempting to stop a white Chevy Corsica, Maryland registration, Alpha– Bravo–Bravo–nine–one– nine, heading west on Church Street."

"Ten-four, Adam 5, 0245 hours."

He pulled out of the parking lot and pushed the gas pedal to the floor in an attempt to catch up to the white Corsica. The vehicle looked pretty beat up and rusty and he noticed when he caught up to it that it was also covered in bumper stickers. He could see that the driver's reactions were sluggish and unpredictable; one moment the driver would be driving in a straight line at a high rate of speed and the next, he would slow down and swerve into the oncoming lane. This guy was going to kill someone if Pat didn't stop him.

The driver threw an object out of the driver's side window, and it almost struck the cruiser's windshield.

The object turned out to be a brown bottle with a silver label. Red and black letters proclaimed the beverage to be Coors Light.

The bottle was still at least half-full when it hit the ground and shattered, the contents exploding all over the roadway in a white flash of foam. At that point, the driver finally decided that it was time to pull over and see what Pat wanted.

When the white Corsica finally pulled over to the side of the road, the passenger's side of the vehicle jumped up onto the curb, bringing the vehicle to a complete stop. Pat radioed dispatch.

"County, the driver's stopped on Church and Twenty-Second Streets. Request a second unit if available. Driver appears to be heavily intoxicated."

As usual, Adam 6 was almost immediately on the airwaves stating he was en route and would be backing him up. As Pat got out of his cruiser to approach the driver, Capstone pulled up and stuck his head out the unit's window, nodding toward the Corsica. "Nice parking job."

Pat approached the passenger side of the vehicle and Capstone stood to the rear in an offset position.

"Driver, turn off your engine," Pat said to the attractive frat boy behind the wheel.

The driver was about twenty or twenty-one years old, and wore a white baseball cap, which was on backwards. The guy had a white T-shirt on, Greek letters on the front advertising his fraternity.

Hank moved around from the rear of the vehicle and, as he looked in the window, he could see that the driver was lighting a cigarette and waited until after the tip glowed red to acknowledge their presence. He took a drag and used his free hand to turn off the engine.

When they looked around the inside of the vehicle, they could see the guy was covered in cigarette ash and there were several empty bottles of Coors Light sitting on the floor.

The driver put down the rear passenger window and tried to speak to them.

"What seems to be the problem, officers?" he asked in a thickly slurred voice. Pat shined his flashlight into his eyes and could see they were bloodshot and had that glassy look about them.

"Have you been drinking tonight, sir?" he asked, anticipating anything but the truth coming out of his mouth. Drunk drivers usually tell officers that they've had two beers, never accounting for the ten shots of whatever else they had.

The driver realized that he had put down the wrong window and corrected the mistake by putting up the rear window and fumbling with the power buttons until the front window went down. The odor of alcohol and tobacco was overpowering. The cigarette the drunken frat boy had lit to cover up the smell of beer merely served to intensify the alcoholic odor.

Pat kept a close eye on the male's hands. He wanted to be absolutely sure he wasn't going to try to start the vehicle or maybe do something even less smart, like grab a weapon. Hank returned to the rear of the vehicle.

"I said, what seems to be the problem tonight, officer?" the male repeated, in a voice that was his attempt to appear sober.

Hank walked up to the driver's side window so he would be able to observe the driver a little better. When the frat boy heard Hank moving to the other side of the vehicle, he turned his head, and asked Hank, "Two of you? What do you need two of you for?"

Hank just smiled and said, "Sir, hope the little frat party was worth it."

The driver didn't acknowledge what Hank had said and instead turned on his interior vehicle light. At that moment Pat saw a sticker that the male had affixed to the interior dashboard of his vehicle. In large black letters on a white background the sticker stated in block letters, "Kill a Queer for Christ."

If this guy had ever had a chance of walking from this stop, it was no longer an option in Pat's mind. He told the male to stay in his vehicle. Hank met his partner near the rear of the Corsica and Pat asked him, "Did you see the sticker on the dashboard?" Hank shook his head no and shined his flashlight into the front seat so he could see the sticker from his position.

Hank looked at Pat and smiled grimly. They both walked back to their positions and in his most official voice Pat ordered, "Sir, step out of your vehicle." The driver ignored them.

"Sir, I will ask you one more time to step out of the vehicle, or we will remove you from the vehicle."

The driver hesitated at first and asked, "For what?"

Hank opened the driver's door for him and pulled him out of the vehicle. The male nearly fell to the ground as he was torn out of his seat. Hank and Pat picked the drunk up off of the ground and leaned him face-first up against the side of the vehicle.

"You guys are assholes, big tough cops. You're nothing without those badges. Fuck you, you fucking faggots."

Pat grabbed the drunk's hands and handcuffed him. The driver was getting very testy and Pat didn't want to wait until he got brave enough to resist arrest to cuff him. He walked the wobbly man back to the rear of his vehicle and pushed his head onto the trunk of his car. As he began to pat him down, he noticed three things almost immediately. First, there was another antigay sticker on the bumper stating "AIDS cures fags." Second, he had a huge cock, measuring at least nine inches. And third, he was hard as a rock.

Pat was checking his right thigh pocket when he felt it almost poking through the waistband of his jeans. In the very same pocket he found a small plastic baggy containing some marijuana. The man protested when Pat pulled it from his pocket.

"I'm holding that for a friend; it's not mine."

"That's original. Never heard that before," Hank said with a laugh.

The frat boy rolled his eyes, knowing that he was screwed. He began to tear up.

"Are you going to cry? Big tough college guy like you, with all these gay-bashing stickers all over your car!"

The man said, "I can put anything I want on this car. It's called freedom of speech! If any faggots tried to grab my junk, I'd kick their asses."

Pat looked at Hank and said, "Hey, partner, you better search him again for me, just in case I missed anything."

After Hank found the lethal weapon the drunk was hiding in his crotch, they placed him in the back of Pat's cruiser.

"Well, I guess he's going to kick our asses," Hank said with a smile.

"Don't some guys get all the breaks?"

While Hank watched their prisoner, Pat searched the Corsica for any other contraband. Under the driver's-side seat he found two things he never thought he would find in their new friend's car: a bottle of Wet and a *Freshmen* magazine still in its wrapper.

"Hank, you got any evidence bags for these?"

The frat boy saw him holding up the magazine and was not happy. He made his feelings known from the backseat of the cruiser.

"Those aren't mine!" he screamed for the world to hear.

"Tell it to someone who will believe it!" Pat responded. He just couldn't help himself.

Hank and Pat looked at each other and shook their heads. If the boy sprouted wood while being handcuffed and searched that was one thing; the fact that he had lube and a *Freshmen* magazine in his car was another thing altogether.

It was very clear that this guy was a closet case of the worst kind. He probably made fun of gay guys while he was with his buddies, but once they were gone he was all about the cock. Pat certainly didn't have any problems with someone being a closet case, since he was one on his job. But he couldn't stand a gay-bashing closet case who was trying to hide it so much that he would put antigay stickers on his car and proclaim AIDS as a cure for homosexuality. Fuck him.

As they finished processing the evidence, they heard someone hitting something. The frat boy was trying to kick out the cruiser's rear window. Pat ran back to his unit and pounded on the roof, yelling, "Yo, knock it off before you break the window!"

"Fuck you. I'm dead. My old man's gonna kill me," he said, crying as he kicked at the window.

Hank ripped open the passenger side of the cruiser, pulled the man upright in his seat and seat-belted him into place.

"I hate college. I only go because my dad makes me. The college is gonna throw me out when they find out I got busted for weed, and then my dad is gonna cut me off," he said, crying like a four-year-old girl.

"Oh, stop," Pat said to him. "You screwed up, not me, and I don't want to hear it."

"Do you know what it's like being someone who just can't fit in?"

He could see where this was going and he didn't want to hear it. Hank closed the cruiser door and got into the front seat.

"I better ride along; God knows what he might try at this point."

After the tow truck came and removed the white Corsica, they headed to the DUI processing center. In order to speed along the processing of drunk drivers, the county paid to establish the drunk driving processing center. It was located right next to the main station.

The only thing the arresting officer had to do at the DUI center was bring the suspect inside. A center worker would do all of the necessary testing.

The frat boy in the rear of the cruiser stopped talking and then passed out. He began to snore.

Hank looked into the back seat and said, "What a mess. I'd feel bad for him if it wasn't for the stickers."

"I'm just going to forget we found the weed. He has enough to deal with and he doesn't need to get tossed out of college on top of it." Pat put his window down and emptied the contents of the little baggy onto the highway. Hank started to chuckle uncontrollably.

"What's so funny?" Pat asked.

"I'm just glad he's not in my cruiser," Hank said.

"What? Why?"

"Not only is he covered in drool, cigarette ash, and spilled booze but he just pissed himself and you have to clean it up," Hank said, as he went from a chuckle to an all-out laugh.

Pat called dispatch and announced that they had one adult male in custody for driving while intoxicated and that they were almost at the DUI center. As the cruiser pulled up to the processing center, Hank looked at his partner and said, "Time to wake Sleeping Beauty!"

"Wonderful," Pat responded.

When Hank opened the rear door, they nearly fell over from the disgusting smell emanating from the backseat. This mess of a man had a string of drool from his mouth to his rock-hard abs, and had urinated all over himself.

The boy felt the blast of air and woke up.

"All right, let's go," Hank said to him.

"Where are we? Who are you?" he asked.

Hank rolled his eyes as he unbuckled the now wet seatbelt. He looked Pat in the eye and said, "I'll never complain about a quiet night again, I swear."

Sergeant Durkin was standing near the entryway, holding the door open. "Got to love them drunks."

"Not really, Sarge. This one's a little messier than I'm used to," Hank complained.

Sergeant Durkin laughed. "Oh look, he even pissed himself too. I'll go get you some paper towels and Mr. Clean to get that just-pissed smell out of your car."

Durkin was quite amused with himself, laughing at Hank, knowing that they would be scrubbing out that backseat for at least an hour.

So, the partners didn't feel too bad when the boy stopped at Sergeant Durkin as they walked by and said, "I'll blow all three of you if you let me go," and then threw up all over Durkin's shoes and pants.

So much for being a closet case, Pat thought to himself.

"Right on my newest god damn uniform!" Durkin screamed.

"Hey, Sarge, I'll go get you some paper towels and Mr. Clean so you can clean that off," Hank chuckled.

The Sergeant sure wasn't laughing anymore, and he shot Hank the evilest of looks.

Pat took the boy to the processing sergeant and said, "He just puked on Sergeant Durkin out there so good luck with this one!"

The sergeant just looked at Pat and chuckled. "Gonna have to check the surveillance camera and save that one for the greatest hits archive."

After the processing sergeant took custody of the frat boy, he led him into the testing room. Hank and Pat went into the bathroom to wash their hands.

They then proceeded to the video area, where officers can observe the tests being administered. When the processing officer attempted to conduct the horizontal gaze nystagmus test, which is a test where the suspect follows a pen with his eyes, the frat boy fell over onto the floor.

"Well, let's go finish these reports," Pat said

"Want to go back to the station after we lock him up?" Hank asked.

"Sure." He watched the EMT who was stationed in the center place the intoxicated man onto a stretcher as the processing officer came into the video room. "I'll have the hospital draw blood for the blood alcohol concentration test; he's too drunk to continue here."

That meant Hank and Pat were free. The processing officer would stay with him until the blood was drawn and secured, so there was no need for them to stick around.

"Let's go get my cruiser first," Hank said, stepping over the puddle of vomit that was left on the ground.

"Yeah, right, after we get the piss off my backseat!" Pat said with a forced smile.

After Pat and Hank picked up Hank's cruiser they went back to the station and found Sergeant Durkin in his tactical uniform.

They guessed he did not have a spare patrol uniform at the station. *I'll have to remember to keep one around just in case,* Pat thought to himself. Ahh, the joys of being a cop….

Chapter Nine
Killer Ambition

IN a different part of the county, a black stretch Lincoln Town Car sped along the highway, surrounded by the Maryland State Police personnel that were assigned to the governor's protection contingent. The governor and his chief of staff were sitting in the backseat of the vehicle contemplating the day's events. They had just come from a political fund-raiser at the Hilton hotel and the governor had another one of his private meetings that the chief of staff so frequently arranged for him. Governor Hanes smiled in the darkness as he recalled the more unorthodox events of the evening.

The governor had entered room 4369 of the Hilton Hotel, led by his chief of staff. The young man that Bill had arranged the meeting with was waiting for them.

"Hello, I'm Governor Hanes," he said, while putting out his right hand to shake.

"Hello, I'm Eddie, Governor Hanes. It's an honor to meet you. May I take your briefcase?"

"No, that's fine; I'll just set it on the dresser here. I understand you want to become a Maryland State Trooper, is that correct?"

"Well, excuse me, gentlemen, I shall leave you two to talk alone," Bill said as he turned around and left the room.

"Yes, sir. I don't want to have a career standing around in hotel lobbies as a security guard for the rest of my life," he replied with a smile.

"Well, as you know, it is very difficult to get accepted into the Maryland State Police Academy. It takes a lot of patience and perseverance."

"Believe me, I know, Governor. I've applied three times and keep getting turned down. They want everyone to have a bachelor's degree, and I only have an associate's degree. I am going to try and finish at a four-year college, but it takes money."

"Well, Eddie, it can pay to have friends in the right places. You know what I mean?"

"I'm not sure, Governor. Do you mean you'll help me get in?"

"Eddie, all I have to do is pick up the phone and you are a cadet in the state police academy. Would you like that?"

"Hell yes, Governor! But why would you be willing to do that for someone you don't even know?"

"Well, as you may know, everything in this world has a price, a cost, that one must pay in order to achieve it. You can have your dream by paying a price for that dream."

"What price is that, Governor? I don't have any money or anything else of value."

"There you're wrong, Eddie. You have something very valuable that I want, and I am willing to pay you for it with my influence."

"What, Governor? What could I possibly have that the governor of Maryland would want?"

"The pure joy of possessing you in bed. I want to make love to you, Eddie. I want to fuck your ass. Does that surprise you?"

Eddie's jaw dropped open in utter shock and after recovering a bit, said, "Excuse me? You wanna fuck me?! And in exchange for that, I can become a Maryland Trooper? Are you serious?"

"Yes, I'm quite serious. I don't have a lot of time to waste, so if you are interested, we need to get at it."

"Governor, do I look gay?"

"What does gay look like, Eddie? Do I look like I fuck cute guys like you?"

Eddie got up to leave and when the governor saw that his bribe was not going to get Eddie out of his clothes, he tried another tack.

"Sit down! Now, this is the way it's going to go down. You are going to let me fuck your ass, or you will never become a cop anywhere. Do you understand? I will call in my police detail right now, and say you assaulted me. What's it going to be?"

Eddie was trapped and he knew it. The fact that Eddie was secretly gay had nothing to do with what was about to happen. He was not going to enjoy this at all, unlike when he fucked the Argentinean hotel-restaurant waiter.

"Okay, Governor. I hope you can live with yourself after this."

As Eddie began to strip, the governor opened his briefcase and pulled out a rubber and lube. He was careful not to let Eddie see anything else in the case. He then put it next to the bed, and took off his clothes.

At first, the governor just sucked Eddie's average-size cock for a few minutes, but what he really wanted was Eddie's well-built ass.

"Turn over," the governor ordered.

Eddie knew what the governor was going to do, and he didn't like it. Eddie considered himself a top only and had never been on the receiving end of a hard-on in the anal area.

"Governor, I really don't want to be fucked. I'm a virgin and would like to stay that way. Just suck my cock if you have to."

"Oh, I'm not going to fuck you, I just want to eat out your ass before you fuck me," lied the governor.

Eddie thought for a moment and decided that he could deal with that. In fact, he liked his ass serviced in that way. Eddie rolled over and even spread his legs a little to make it easier for his ass cheeks to be spread.

After Eddie rolled over, the governor began kissing and licking Eddie's ass while at the same time reaching over and opening his briefcase. As Eddie began to actually enjoy himself, the governor in one swift motion injected Eddie's neck with the powerful combination of drugs that he used to incapacitate his victims.

Eddie screamed out slightly as he felt the prick of the needle enter his neck, but soon found himself unable to speak or move. He was floating in a drug-induced aura where he felt no pain and very little pleasure.

The governor now had his victim just the way he liked. He slipped on the rubber and, without lube, entered his victim's ass. When he had finished, it was time for the murderer to do what came too easily for him to do: kill his victim.

Hanes removed a belt from his briefcase and wrapped it around Eddie's neck, jerking his head back. He tightened the belt and strangled Eddie without even a second thought while his cock was still inside him. He grew even harder once again as he murdered his victim. Even in his semi-comatose state, Eddie struggled for life, believing he could overcome the odds. Eddie failed and died at the age of twenty-four – another victim of a monster that few knew.

The governor quickly got dressed, packed up all the evidence (including the used rubber) and was about to leave the room when he remembered. The belt. He must get the belt. Hanes turned around and removed the belt from Eddie's pants, rolled it up, and put it into his briefcase. The governor noted a terrible taste in his mouth from Eddie's sweaty ass, and quickly rinsed his mouth out in the sink.

"The things I do for ass," snorted the governor as he spit out the water post-gargle.

The governor left the room and knocked on the door of the adjoining room and told Bill he was ready to leave. Bill radioed the police detail to meet them in the lobby and to have the limo ready.

As Governor Hanes and Bill exited the elevator, they were met by the state police detail. They quickly left the hotel and got into the limousine.

The chief of staff stared out his window, watching the passing neon signs that lit up the city at night. Hanes hit the button to raise the privacy shield between the rear occupants and the driver and one of his bodyguards. Next, he hit the button that activated the device that made it almost impossible to record any conversations inside of the vehicle compartment. The governor sat in his seat with a look of ecstasy on his face.

"I love these little get-togethers. Don't you, Bill?"

"Yes, sir. This was one of our more successful fund-raisers," the chief of staff said half-heartedly.

"Yeah, that too," the governor said with a smirk that could not be seen in the darkness. "You know I talked to the party chairman about you, right? It looks good for you, Bill. As long as I give my blessing the party will back you for that congressional seat you've got your eye on," he continued. "It serves that little prick Mendelssohn right to lose his seat to a protégé of mine."

The chief of staff's feelings of disgust were erased by what the governor had just told him. His goal would soon be achieved. If he played ball just a little bit longer, he would be a congressman and then get away from this … man. Protégé indeed!

There was something the chief of staff wanted to discuss with the governor regarding the risks they were taking at these little get-togethers. It wasn't smart for the governor to be meeting tricks at such high-profile events.

The governor's sexual proclivities were top secret; the only people who knew of the governor's taste for young men were the chief of staff, the governor, and the young men themselves. The state police contingent was always kept at a distance to ensure that no one got too close to the truth, while at the same time providing a wonderful cover.

"What's bothering you, Bill?"

"Nothing, Governor. I'm just excited to hear the party is going to back me."

"I said they agreed to back you if I gave my blessing, Bill, but they're not doing a god damned thing yet," the governor warned.

"I'm not just going to let you move on until I'm sure we've got everything under control, understood?" he continued.

"Sir, I've been with you for what? Eight years now? I've done all that you asked and never complained. What makes you think that I'd say anything about your little trysts? That would be political suicide for me and I've worked way too hard to get the nod from the party to have my own political office," the now agitated chief of staff said.

With that the governor picked up his briefcase and removed the newly acquired belt. He struck the chief of staff in the face with the metal buckle, drawing blood.

"If you ever bring that up again, you'll have a lot more to worry about than the Republicans giving you their political blessing," the governor said, leaning over the chief of staff menacingly while gripping the leather belt that had now become a weapon.

The governor sat back in his seat and placed the belt in his lap; he was still stroking his new trophy when the black Town Car pulled into the driveway of the governor's mansion. He shoved it back into his briefcase.

"Goodnight, Bill. See you tomorrow at the photo shoot."

One of the state police bodyguards opened the governor's car door and signaled it was all clear to exit.

The state police officer looked at the chief of staff's face and asked, "Are you all right, sir?" The chief of staff put his handkerchief over his freshly bloodied lip and replied, "Yeah.

Just a knick. Shit happens."

The officer closed the door and the car pulled away, taking the chief of staff to his home.

THE next day the governor was doing a photo shoot with his family. It was one of those "we love our daddy/husband/governor" things that was necessary whenever a controversial piece of legislation was being introduced by a political figure.

The governor and his wife were dressed in their Sunday best and their nine-year-old daughter had been groomed by the staff makeup people to prep for the shoot. The chief of staff was on the phone dealing with one of the many daily crises that happened in the governor's mansion as his son stood by his side and watched, hoping to learn as much as he could from his father. The chief of staff's son had political ambitions even greater than those of his father. His son was a muscular boy with the frame of a track star, nineteen years of age, with brown hair and piercing hazel eyes. He was attending the University of Maryland to work toward his political science degree. He wanted to follow in his father's footsteps and make a career of politics.

This worried his father to a great extent, as he had sacrificed so much, both physically and morally, to get where he was. *Oh, the cost.* He had no wish to let his son do the same in order to get ahead in the corrupt world of politics, and often attempted to dissuade him from such a life in favor of becoming a lawyer.

The governor sat with his wife and daughter at his side while the photographer did his best to make the man look like a caring leader and loving husband and father.

The chief of staff finished dealing with the crisis of the moment and made notes in his PDA.

"Governor, the department of transportation is threatening a strike if we don't meet with them today."

"Thank the good lord it's summer and we don't need them to plow snow! Let them wait. Sunshine doesn't need to be shoveled," replied the governor, in between clicks of the high-speed camera.

"Excuse me, Governor. I've taken about a two-dozen pictures and have a couple of real nice shots. Unless there is something else, I'll get on the development of the film."

"That's fine, George. Thank you. Let me see them as soon as you have them."

"Yes, sir."

The governor's wife stopped smiling and shot her husband an evil glare.

"If I have to do one more photo shoot while some faggot photographer stares at you, I'm going to scream," she said through a clenched jaw.

"What's a faggot, Daddy?" asked the governor's daughter innocently.

"It's a bad word we should never use, honey," said the governor in his most fatherly tone as his wife took her daughter's hand and exited the room.

Bill's son stood there with his eyes widened slightly upon hearing the governor's wife. He tried not to stare at her as she left the room.

The governor picked up on the boy's discomfort at what his wife had said and walked up to him, extending his hand and introducing himself.

"Hello, I'm Governor Hanes. I believe we met a few years back when your father started working for me. You've grown into quite the young man since then," he said, as he firmly shook the boy's hand.

"She's quite a woman," said the boy politely.

"She never was one for politics and the life that comes with it," the governor replied.

The chief of staff hung up his phone again and walked over to the two men who were already engaged in conversation.

"Sir, the chairman of the DOT said we have until midnight tonight to come to the bargaining table. He also said if the DOT strikes you'll lose a lot of the support you have from the state senate when it comes time to vote on your upcoming Death with Dignity legislation," the chief of staff said flatly.

"Fine. Call him back and tell him he's got until eight tonight to be here, then he can kiss my ass," the governor said, slightly annoyed.

Young Daniel was amazed at the inner workings of politics behind the scenes. "So this is how it really works, sir?" asked the inexperienced boy.

"Not exactly what they teach you in civics class, is it son?" replied the governor.

The chief of staff walked away, speaking on his cell phone to the unseen chairman of the DOT. Bill noticed that the governor had taken a liking to his son, from the firm handshake to the governor putting his hand on his shoulder as they talked about politics behind the scenes. These were classic moves for the governor when he was attempting to ingratiate himself with a young man he liked.

The governor put both of his hands on the boy's shoulders and quietly whispered, "I know your dad doesn't want you in politics. Are you sure this is the type of life you want?"

"Absolutely, sir," said the boy excitedly.

"Well then, I have an internship available in my office for the summer. It's hard work and there are a lot of things you would have to do for me. The kind of things that they don't teach you in civics class," said the governor with a smile.

The governor's eyes went to the boy's belt and what lay beneath it.

The boy shrunk back a little bit. Inexperienced or not, he had the feeling that the governor wasn't talking about filing.

"Thank you, sir. I'll think about it," the now apprehensive boy said, as he awkwardly walked toward his father.

"Dad, I don't feel good. I'm going to head home and lie down."

Daniel was unaware that his father had overheard the exchange and felt very uncomfortable himself.

"WHAT was that about, Governor?" asked the chief of staff.

"I want to try and help your boy out. I offered him an internship at the governor's mansion for the summer. I would love to have him around, you know, to let him see how things work," said the governor as he stared at the chief of staff's now healing wound. "It would do wonders for his résumé in the future, and it's worth the sacrifice of his summer to work for me."

With that the governor walked away. Bill watched from the second-floor window as his son got into his car and drove away from the mansion. *That sick son of a bitch had better keep his hands off his kid!*

The governor was in his office seated at his desk reviewing his calendar for the following week, when his mind began to wander to the nineteen-year-old boy that had stood before him. Those beautiful hazel eyes; that warm, moist grip; the way the blazer hung off of the boy's muscular shoulders. The governor was now stroking himself, thinking of the things he would have loved to do to the prospective intern's ass.

The governor hit the button under his desk that closed his door and then told his secretary he could not be bothered for a half-hour. The governor closed his eyes and leaned back in his leather chair, smelling the hand that the boy had gripped while unzipping his pants and taking out his now rock-hard cock with the other.

The governor thought of bending the hot young male with the runner's build over his desk and pulling on his hair as he fucked his virgin ass bareback, hearing him yelp as the governor penetrated him and then the warm feeling as he spurted into the boy's hot, tight hole. The governor exploded in ecstasy all over his hand and onto his shirt, sending pulse after pulse of cum in various directions.

He began to wipe up his spilled seed as he formulated how he would get the boy alone so he could fuck him, and fuck him hard.

The governor had his next fuck in mind and he knew he couldn't let the boy's father know his true intentions. After all, the boy had political ambitions. Maybe he'd just keep him around a little longer than the rest, the governor thought as he zipped himself back up.

The governor buzzed his secretary to let her know he was now available.

"Yes, sir. The chief of staff is here to see you," she said.

"Send him in."

"Governor, the chairman of the DOT is here," Bill said.

The chief of staff led the labor secretary and the chairman of the DOT into the office and left the governor to take care of some state business for a change.

WHEN Bill got back to his office, his secretary told him that two uniformed police officers were waiting for him.

"Sir, they don't have an appointment, but they said it was official police business and that they had to speak with you."

"It's okay, Nancy. Thank you."

As he walked into the office, St. James and Capstone stood up and shook his hand.

"Good afternoon, sir. I'm Officer St. James and my partner is Officer Capstone, and we are with the Prince George's County Police Department."

"Prince George's County? This is a surprise. My secretary said you stated this visit was official police business. What can I do for you?" Bill asked cordially

St. James pulled out a printout from a DMV record.

"A witness at a crime scene gave us a registration plate belonging to the only strange, out-of- place vehicle that was present at the time," he responded.

"Well, really, you know as well as I do, that witnesses give wrong information all the time to the police. Maybe not on purpose, but the eyes and memory play tricks on people. I'm sure they got the plate wrong, reversed a number or something like that."

"Mr. Dugan, the plate was 'Maryland One.' It would be pretty hard to screw that up, wouldn't you say? And as you know, the only car in the state with that registration plate is the governor's personal limo."

"Really? Is the witness sure of the plate number? Just exactly what kind of a crime occurred in the area in which the governor might have been? Of course, just because his car might have been there, does not mean the governor was in the car."

"Frankly, sir, before we get into that, I need to know who attended the fund-raiser that was held at the Hilton hotel last night, and who rode in the governor's limo," Pat said in a very official voice.

Bill was getting more nervous by the second. He wasn't a moron; he knew what these two cops were doing.

"Gentlemen, you will have to get that from the state police protective detail liaison. I'm not cleared to give out just who rides in the limo and who doesn't. That would violate all kinds of security protocols and such. Now if you will excuse me I have a looming DOT strike to deal with," Bill replied while standing up behind his desk in a gesture to the police that it was time to leave.

Hank and Pat almost walked out of the office, knowing that they were being stonewalled but not knowing why, when Pat turned back around and said, "Sir, I'll need the name and number of the state police liaison so we can get that information," he said, looking at the now sweating chief of staff.

"See my secretary. She will give it to you. Have a safe day, gentlemen," Bill replied while hitting the button under his desk that would close the door behind the two nosy officers.

THE chief of staff collapsed back into his chair, sighing with relief that the two officers had left. St. James and Capstone obtained the contact information from the secretary stationed outside of the door and left the mansion.

They both got into Pat's cruiser and waited until they cleared the security gate before saying anything.

"Pat, that guy's hiding something," Capstone said.

"Obviously! I mean, he basically threw us out after we told him we needed to know who was in the car," St. James said. He was irritated but intrigued.

"Do you think they saw something or, maybe worse, had something to hide?" Capstone asked.

"That guy was hiding something, that's for sure. I'm going to contact this state trooper and find out who was in the car when it left the hotel. It was the only private car seen leaving the hotel at the time of the murder. The room came back to a phony registration and we have only this lead. You do some background on that chief of staff, and I'll let homicide know what we have," he said.

Chapter Ten
Blood is Thicker Than Politics

ABOUT an hour after Pat and Hank left the Chief of Staff's office, Pat was just finishing a phone call to the State Police personal protection liaison when Hank rejoined him.

"The only people in the car were the driver, a second state trooper in the front passenger seat, and the chief of staff and the governor in the backseat. Apparently for the past few months the governor has requested no troopers ride in the back of the limo, and no increase of close-in security," he told Hank.

This was getting very weird. A very prominent government official, who was in the middle of trying to pass one of the most inflammatory pieces of legislation ever to be introduced in the Maryland House and Senate, did not want increased protection when he traveled. Why was that? They couldn't figure it out, so Hank and Pat went to the homicide detective and shared their findings.

"Hey, boys. Good to see you both. I have to go to the coroner's office, and if you come with me, it'll be a good experience for you both. You can ride with me," said Detective Sheffield.

It was a short ride to the morgue and the police parking spot was open.

"Good Morning, Doc," said Detective Sheffield as they entered the county forensics lab.

"Detective, good to see you. Who are the rookies?" asked the older man with a beard wearing a name tag that read "Dr. Paul Mason, Forensic Pathologist."

"Officers Patrick St. James and Hank Capstone; they are the assisting uniforms on the detail," answered Detective Sheffield. "Hey, Doc, let's give the boys the full run, shall we?" chuckled Sheffield.

"I wish I could. Nothing like seeing rookies lose their lunch as I cut open the ribcage. However, today we have fifteen waiting bodies from an apartment fire, so I'm swamped," said the doctor.

The doctor led the three men over to his desk and pulled a file from a huge pile on his desk.

"This guy was strangled with some type of strap; note the ligature marks near the clavicles and the crushed Adam's apple," stated the doctor.

"Any defensive wounds? Was there a struggle, or was it a total surprise?" asked St. James.

"Nothing at all, but according to the toxicology results that just came back, there was enough morphine and Xanax in this guy's blood to knock out an elephant," said the doctor.

"Ah, so even if he wanted to resist, he couldn't have," observed Detective Sheffield.

"There had also been some recent sexual activity and I'm not sure if he was totally willing. There is some rectal tearing," continued the doctor. "There is one other thing, however. This victim reminded me of another male that came through here a week or two back; recent sexual activity, ligature marks, and a high amount of prescription narcotics in the blood with the same cause of death as this young man. Strangulation. So we ran the DNA of the hair follicle found at the first scene and did a comparison test with the DNA of the saliva you found on the bathroom mirror from the second crime scene and, voila, they match."

"So we got a serial killer on our hands. Is that what you're saying, Doc?" asked Sheffield.

"It's your job to determine that, not mine," said the doc, pointing his finger at the detective as he walked away.

"Two guys with nothing in common except liking cock, and they're killed the same way. Smells like that god damned clan thing again! Didn't all of those dumb bastards die in that blast, St. James?" asked the detective rhetorically.

St. James and Hank exchanged worried glances at the prospect of another gay predator. Worse yet, had one of the Milford clan survived? They also exchanged the "homophobic dickhead" look as they heard the liking cock comment made by Sheffield.

"I'll put a copy of these reports in the file, you two go back onto whatever the shift command has you on," said the detective as he walked away while dialing his cell phone.

"What do you think, Pat? The clan?" asked Hank

"Don't know what to think, Hank. We don't have enough information right now," he answered.

Pat kept looking at a photo in the dead man's morgue jacket. It was a photo of the victim's personal effects. It was standard procedure to take a picture of all items that the deceased had with them when they were brought in.

"Hank, look at this. Four of the belt loops look like they were torn off in a hurry. It even ripped the pants," he said.

"So maybe he was so ready to be fucked he tore it off in a fit of lust," responded Hank.

"Okay then, horn ball, where's the belt?"

"Maybe he didn't wear one the day he was killed," Hank said dismissively.

"Then why did he have a cell phone in its case with him? I mean, if you keep a loose one in your pocket, now that's different. But this one is still in its little nylon Velcro case. It had to hang on something," he said, intrigued but not sure of what it meant.

"I guess it depends on where it was found on the body," Hank shot back.

"According to the forensics guys, it was under his front right pelvic area right where the last loop is ripped. That's where it fell off when whoever did this ripped off his belt," Pat said.

"Where do you think the belt is now?"

"It doesn't look like they found it," he answered.

"Well, let's get this to Sheffield," Hank stated.

"I don't know. Let's save this one until we are sure. Besides, Mr. "liking cock" would love to get credit for figuring that little gem out," Pat said with a grin.

BACK in the governor's mansion, the chief of staff had recovered from what he thought was a successful stonewalling of the police. Little did he know, he had actually just poured gasoline on a spark that was quickly becoming a firestorm. It was 10:30 p.m. when the governor finished meeting with the chairman of the DOT. They had yelled, screamed, threatened and postured their way to an agreement; by the time it was all said and done they had finished a fine bottle of vanilla cognac and smoked several Cuban cigars.

The crisis was over. The DOT agreed not to strike in exchange for a "no co-pay" on their health insurance and a five percent pay raise. The governor's legislation was all but assured to pass now. The DOT chairman and the labor secretary were very politically connected and had given their assurances that the deal would be done if the governor agreed to these concessions.

The governor picked up his phone and dialed the extension for the chief of staff's office. Bill was in his office awaiting final word on the DOT deal. It was his duty to call a press conference if the DOT decided to strike and to have the spin doctors do their best to try and save the governor's ass.

"Hello, Bill. It's me. Come on down to my office and have a drink," the slightly intoxicated governor said.

"Sir, it's late and I have to get home to my family," Bill replied.

"Nonsense! One drink won't hurt. Get your ass over here, now!" demanded the governor.

BILL entered the governor's office and poured himself a drink into a large glass.

"I love how quiet this place is after everyone leaves," observed the governor, a half-smoked cigar in his mouth.

Task Force

"So, your legislation is going to pass, I take it?" Bill asked, while guzzling down his fine vanilla cognac and pouring himself another.

"Overwhelmingly!" shouted the governor.

"After this bill passes, will I have what I want?" Bill asked as he sucked down his second large glass of cognac.

"What's that, Bill? Hmmm? To be a congressman?" asked the governor, turning toward him.

"Yes, sir. The primary is only six months away and I need to file petitions and prepare a campaign if I'll have any chance of winning."

"I'll tell you what, Bill. Have your son report here on Monday morning, and you can start your campaign for Congress on Wednesday. He will help take some of the workload and stress off of my staff as you campaign," said the governor.

Bullshit!! You psycho, you want me to let you fuck my son for Republican backing, thought Bill.

It was becoming very clear that the governor had no intentions of helping Bill become a congressman. He had been dangling this juicy steak in front of him for the past three years, knowing there was no way he could let Bill leave his sight.

"Are you saying the party gave the nod and I can expect the funding and their full backing, Governor?"

"I'm saying you're set right after I have a replacement for you, Bill. Namely your son," the governor said in a patronizing voice.

At this point Bill felt a knot forming in his stomach. He poured one final glass of cognac and sucked it down faster than the first two.

He could not believe his ears. This nauseating man was basically saying that if he offered his son's ass up as a sacrifice, he'd fulfill Bill's wish to be a congressman. The question was whether or not he was willing to sacrifice his son for a lifelong ambition.

He grabbed the internship application off the governor's desk and walked out of the office without saying a word to the inebriated man that had just attempted to bribe him with a congressional seat.

He had served this man beyond faithfully for eight years now. He had done some things he was not proud of to get into the position he was in, but he could not stomach the thought of this man seducing his son and possibly killing him.

He got into his car and began to drive home, occasionally mumbling to himself about what he could do to the governor if he wanted to, how much damage he could cause. He was tired of recruiting boys for the governor to fuck! He had become a high-price pimp, keeping his boss's sexual appetite satiated. He was aware that a couple of the boys that he had recruited had turned up dead as well, but he tried to convince himself it was all unrelated and merely coincidental. He had almost believed that until the Hilton hotel trick. He had gotten a security guard who had inquired about the Maryland State Police to meet with the governor; the guard was exactly what the governor had set his eye on since walking into the hotel.

"Bill, that one," the governor had said as they walked by the security officer who was standing his post in the hotel lobby.

He had approached the guard and told him that the governor wanted to meet with him personally in order to thank him for his cooperation with his State Police detail regarding his security. The young, inexperienced security officer was overwhelmed by the request and had ambitions of becoming a Maryland State Trooper, so he complied.

The governor met him in the hotel room and began to talk about the Maryland State Police and how helpful the governor's office could be in getting him a position, and that's when Bill left the room. He could not stand to see another young man corrupted by greed and sexual lust.

He was trying to deal with his own sense of guilt at having played any part in the earlier event and had been reliving the entire scenario in his head. Being deep in thought, he didn't notice that he was now on Church Street, and had missed the turn to his residence. He was also quite drunk from all of the alcohol he had quickly imbibed to kill the feelings of hatred and disgust that he had been feeling toward the governor. He knew he shouldn't drink like that and then drive.

He drove his white BMW through an intersection near a 7-Eleven; the same 7-Eleven where Shawn worked, which usually had a couple of police cruisers there on and off throughout the night.

HANK and Pat had just pulled into the 7-Eleven parking lot to get their nightly cups of coffee, when Pat saw the car first. It had nearly collided with a vehicle that was entering the intersection, and the driver of that vehicle hit the brakes just in time to avoid a collision.

Hank and Pat pulled out of the 7-Eleven's parking lot to pursue the reckless driver as they activated their lights and sirens and caught up to the vehicle.

"County, I have a white BMW sedan traveling south on Church Street bearing Maryland registration Gulf–Oscar–Victor Charlie–Oscar–Sierra, one occupant."

"Ten-four, Adam 5. Will Adam 6 be joining you?" asked the dispatcher sarcastically.

"Ten-four, County. Adam 6 will assist," said Hank, smiling. Most of the department knew if one of them made a stop the other one would be there to back him up.

The white BMW stopped on the side of the road without incident. Pat got out of his patrol vehicle and walked up to the lone occupant's window. The heavily tinted window went down and the pungent odor of alcohol cut through the night air.

"Good to see you again, Officer St. James," said the chief of staff cordially.

"Yes, sir. You're a ways from Annapolis now. Do you know why we pulled you over?" he asked.

"No idea. Don't you have more important things to do than tie up my life?" asked the inebriated driver impatiently.

"You went through that red light and almost caused an accident and now I can smell that you've been drinking; how much have you had tonight, sir?"

"One or two. I'm not drunk. Don't you have real criminals to be out there chasing?" yelled Bill, knowing that he was screwed.

He knew he'd had way too much to drink, and he knew he should not be driving. Bill had a lot of things on his mind when he got behind that wheel and drove off from the governor's mansion. The sound of that struggle back at the Hilton when the young security guard had the syringe emptied into his neck and the look he must have had on his face as the governor raped him haunted Bill every waking and sleeping moment.

"I'm going to need you to take some field sobriety tests, sir," Pat said, instantly snapping Bill back to reality.

In response to St. James' statement, he threw open the car door, hitting him in the left leg. Pat was knocked off balance. Capstone was on the other side of the vehicle and ran over to help his partner. Capstone grabbed Bill, who began to scream at Pat, and slammed him up against the side of his white BMW.

"What the hell is your problem?" Pat shouted at the man after regaining his balance.

"My problem? What the hell do you mean what's my problem?" the chief of staff said as he struggled to break free from Capstone's grip.

"I'm going to kick your ass, then I'm going to have you both fired!" Bill screamed as Hank slammed handcuffs onto the struggling man's wrists.

"We'll just add resisting arrest and threat of assault to your expanding list of charges, then. So keep talking, smart guy," he said with a smirk on his face. "I'm sure your boss will love reading all about it in the morning papers!"

Both Hank and Pat knew this man had connections with power, possibly enough power to do exactly what the man was threatening to do, but, unfortunately for Bill, he picked the wrong two officers to try and threaten or blackmail. They had dealt with this before, and they knew they would come out on top even if this man did try to screw them over.

Capstone looked the man square in the eye and said, "So you're saying if we arrest you, you're going to have us fired? I'll just have to give my friend at the newspaper a call. I'm sure they'd love to blaze the headline on the front page: 'Governor's Chief of Staff arrested for DUI and official oppression'."

He shoved the man into the back of his cruiser and slammed the door shut.

"We have all the luck, don't we, Hank?" Pat asked, shaking his head.

THE governor's chief of staff knew he was through in politics before he really even began to set upon a path that might lead to his own public election. After this arrest made the newspaper, no one would back him in a congressional run.

The officers got into Pat's cruiser and radioed that they had one in custody for DUI, and that they were bringing him in for processing.

"What if I could help you with what you asked me about earlier today?" asked Bill, through the partition that separated the cruiser's operator from its rear occupants.

"We already know who was in the limo, sir," Pat responded.

"Yeah, you're a day late and more than a dollar short on that one," Hank chimed in.

"That's not what I'm talking about."

They tried not to show too much interest, as they didn't want to give this man the upper hand in his obvious attempt at negotiating his way out of being arrested.

Pat pretended to be annoyed and asked, "So then what are you are talking about?"

"I'm talking about a deal. First of all; I want a lawyer present before we talk about this any more. I want immunity from prosecution, this arrest to go away, and no mention to the press of this incident!" said Bill defiantly.

"I can't make any deals like that, especially if I don't know what you're talking about," Pat answered.

"Then I suggest you get Michael Jenkins out of bed and get his ass down to the station right now," said the chief of staff. "What I have will make you two clowns sergeants, and the DA the next governor of Maryland."

Michael Jenkins was the county DA, and Pat knew he could get through to him due to who the defendant was. An on-call assistant would not need to respond.

"I have his number in my cell phone. We can call him when we get back to your little stationhouse," said the chief of staff.

Hank and Pat both knew they had something big on their hands. The rest of the ride was quiet, until they pulled into the DUI processing center.

"What are you doing?" asked the chief of staff

"We are going to process you for DUI, and then we'll call the DA. Just in case you decide to clam up, I'm going to make sure this case is handled right," he said.

The chief of staff looked at St. James with his mouth wide open.

"Do you guys realize what I am offering you? I know you guys are new on the job, but think about who I am and the information that I possess that will help your careers."

"Look, you still get booked. That's how the process works. When it comes time for prosecution that's when the DA does what he does, so let's get this over with, shall we? Then you get to make your call," Capstone said.

"I strongly urge you to contact your supervisor now, before we go any further. You have no idea what information I am in possession of, and any DA worth his salt will gladly trade this drunk bust for what I have," Bill said sternly.

Pat looked at Hank and nodded. Hank picked up the mic.

"Adam 5 requesting Adam 10 go to channel two ASAP, County."

"Ten-four, Adam 5. Copy, Adam 10?"

"Switching over now, County," responded Durkin.

"Adam 10 from Adam 5, request you meet us at the DUI processing center ASAP."

"Ten-four, en route."

AS the chief of staff was seated outside the Breathalyzer room, he silently considered calling the governor directly and asking him to use his clout to take care of this problem instead of ruining his political career and possibly his life. As Durkin entered the room, he changed his mind.

"What's up, guys?" asked the sergeant.

"We just popped this guy for DUI and resisting. He happens to be the chief of staff for the governor of Maryland, and says he has information that he will give to us in exchange for not pressing the charges we have on him. He also says that his information will make us all famous or some shit if we forget the arrest. He has requested the DA himself respond down here to listen and guarantee that no charges will be pressed against him."

"What kind of information?"

"No idea, Sarge. He won't go any further without the DA being present. He also insisted we ask you to respond here when we said we would process him first."

Durkin walked over to the chief of staff. "So, what type of information do you have? We need at least that much before I allow the DA to be called. This is not open for discussion. Take it or leave it."

At the prospect of ratting out his boss, Bill's tongue felt as if it was made of lead and the knot in his stomach returned. Everything that happened earlier in the night hit him like a locomotive smashing into a horse cart. The chief of staff touched his lip where the potential scar was and began to think of the three boys the governor had likely killed and the roll he had played in all of that. After tonight, Bill had his son to think about also.

"I have information on at least three murders that will make national headlines, and that is all I am going to say without the DA present," Bill answered.

The sergeant turned around to Pat and said, "Put a call in to the DA and tell him what we have. Request that he respond to the detective bureau instead of here."

Durkin turned back to Bill. "If you're bullshitting us, I will personally charge you with false report of a crime and anything else I can think up. Do we understand each other?"

"Yes. You'll see that what I have is worth far more than a DUI bust," Bill responded.

MICHAEL Jenkins showed up at the station within an hour; his hair was a mess and he hadn't exactly dressed like an elected DA should.

"Bill, what's this all about?" asked Jenkins. "I heard you were running for Congress. Now this? There's nothing I can do about this DUI if that's what this is about," stated the DA.

"Fuck the DUI, Mike. First of all, do you think I would bother you at this late hour for something like that? Let me make this known: I want immunity from all prosecution that will result from the information I have and I also want immunity from this stupid DUI and whatever else those two cops are going to tack on," Bill said with some disdain.

"That's quite an order, Bill. What I can or cannot do for you depends on what this is about," Mike stated. "Officer St. James said you had information about three murders? Was that all bullshit to get me down here to quash this arrest, or what?"

Bill smiled and leaned toward the prosecutor. He said one word and one word only:

"Governor."

St. James, Capstone, Durkin, and the homicide detective smiled from ear to ear and looked at one another as they sat behind the two-way mirror that separated the interview room and the observation room.

"I knew it!" Pat exclaimed.

"Calm down, kid. Who knows what he's talking about and if he can even deliver. I've been through this before. Let's see what he says," said the duty detective who had joined the officers in the observation room.

"The governor?" repeated the now very interested DA.

"Yes, Mike. I hear you have three unsolved homicides in your county, all related of course. The boys who were drugged by syringe, raped, and murdered. Let's see the immunity agreement counselor," said Bill.

"Whoa, hold on here. First off, did you kill these guys and the governor knows it?" asked the skeptical DA.

"No, but I know who did and I know how you can prove it," said Bill.

"Well, let's wait until your lawyer arrives, then you two can look over the immunity agreement," said the DA as he exited and joined the others in the observation room.

"OKAY, guys. What the hell is he talking about?" asked Jenkins.

"Three guys all drugged and strangled in hotel rooms; they all had anal intercourse before being murdered, but no semen was left behind. One was found just a few hours ago at the local Hilton hotel, where, I might add, the governor was present with his chief of staff," answered the homicide detective. "We have one blond hair, a partial print, some DNA. All three were strangled or smothered. We couldn't figure out what the killer was using to strangle them with until we noticed all three victims' belts were missing. Today's murder has the same details," Sergeant Durkin added.

"Okay. His hair isn't blond, so we can be pretty sure he isn't the killer. Do you think he had a role in the murders?" asked the DA.

"Sir, we can't be sure of anything right now; this may be our biggest break in the case," the detective said.

"Do you think you can identify a potential suspect without the information that this guy possesses?"

"Not with what we have," the homicide detective responded.

"Okay. We'll offer him conditional immunity and hold him as a material witness using your DUI and resisting-arrest charges. That should stick for a little bit," said Jenkins. He left and entered the room that was now occupied by Bill and his attorney.

"Hello, counselor. You know how this works, right? I've got a conditional immunity offer in my briefcase. The whole thing hinges on your client not being the killer or participating in the actual killing. Do we understand each other?" asked Mike Jenkins.

The defense attorney whispered in his client's ear, and shook his head in agreement.

"We have a deal. Nothing here is on the record until that agreement is signed, agreed?" asked the defense attorney.

"Then let's sign now. There is no such thing as off the record; this is a yes-or-no- situation, period," said the DA. He was slightly annoyed at the delaying tactic the defense attorney was trying to use.

All interested parties signed off on the agreement and the homicide detective entered the room with St. James in tow; Capstone and Durkin watched from behind the mirrored glass.

The cameras and audio recording devices were turned on. Each man in the room identified himself, and Bill began his story.

"My name is William Dugan. I am the chief of staff for the governor of Maryland, and in exchange for immunity, I have agreed to give certain information that I am in possession of regarding the murder of at least one man. Present with me, in addition to the DA and police, is my personal attorney, Benjamin Dorsey, who is advising me."

Chapter Eleven
Baiting the Rattrap

"To begin with, I have worked for Governor Hanes for eight years and not all of them have been happy ones. To the world, Hanes is a happily married man with children, a successful politician who serves the people of Maryland as Governor. He is a doctor and therefore a well-educated man. This is what the public sees. The real truth is that Governor Hanes is an adulterer who likes to have sex with young men. It is more than likely that Hanes has murdered at least one of the men with whom he has had sex. It was more than likely Hanes who killed the security officer at the Hilton a few hours ago after having had sex with him."

"Mr. Dugan, do you realize what you are saying?" asked the DA.

"Of course I do! This isn't something that one would just make up in order to get out of a drunk-driving bust!"

"How long has Hanes been having sex with men?"

"As long as I have known him, although his taste has changed over the years. He now prefers them younger and younger."

"Tell us in detail about your visit to the Hilton hotel located in Prince George's County, Maryland, last night," requested the DA.

As Dugan answered the question regarding the Hilton, the eyes of everyone in the room got wider and wider. No one could believe that the governor might be a murderer, but here sat a man who was close to the governor alleging that very thing. As the DA listened, he saw visions of higher political office dancing in his head. This was the type of case that made careers and changed personal history. Even the detective could picture himself on the evening national news relaying salacious details about the murders to the public and, not long after, being promoted to lieutenant.

"Holy hell! You two stepped in shit again, and came up with the golden idol," said Durkin to Capstone.

"Sure looks that way, Sarge. Just look at Pat in there. He can't believe what he's hearing. In fact, no one would believe this if it wasn't happening right in front of us."

"Well, get ready to be a media star once again, Capstone. When all this goes public, there will be a shit storm, the likes of which this county and state have never seen," observed Durkin. "Better call the chief and inform her in case she wants to respond down here to review this case now. She hates to be blindsided by the media," Durkin ordered.

When the chief of staff finished giving up his boss, the DA asked, "You know you will have to testify in front of the Grand Jury as well as at trial about all of this? Your testimony will be key to tying the governor to the murders. You are lucky that this information did not come to light via a different avenue, or you would find yourself being charged as an accomplice to murder."

"We realize that. This is the reason that he is coming forward with all of this," said Bill's attorney.

"Well, not totally," added Bill.

"What do you mean, not totally?" asked the DA.

"I'm doing it to protect my son as well. The governor has selected him for his next fuck, and I am damn sure he is not going to succeed as long as I am alive."

"How do you know that he's after your son?" asked the DA.

"He ordered me to bring my son to him Monday morning to serve as a summer intern in exchange for party backing for my proposed run for Congress."

COUNTY Police Chief Rachel Morgan arrived as the interview ended. The interview was immediately typed up by the stenographer so that it could be signed and witnessed. Armed with this information, the DA called a special meeting that included the Chief of Police and Homicide supervisors. Because of the nature of the crimes and the success St. James and Capstone had before, both rookie officers were invited.

"Okay, ladies and gentlemen, we have a major crime spree here by the Governor of Maryland and we need to handle this case right. No fuckups, understand? Not one word of this investigation can be relayed to anyone except those in this group," stated the DA.

The Police Chief nodded her head and asked, "You're not going to the Grand Jury with just the statement of a political hack, are you?"

"No. We are going to launch a full investigation and build a case from the ground up. We think we know who the murderer is, and it's now our job to gather as much evidence to support the indictment as we can. When this hits the press, the eyes of the nation will be upon us all and a lot of very powerful people are gonna come gunning for us. Remember, the governor has ties to the White House and the Speaker of the House. We need to be ready for this and not screw it up. Suggestions, anyone," asked the DA.

"Would Dugan be willing to assist us in setting the governor up?" asked the Homicide chief.

"I'm sure he would. It's not like he has much choice in this matter. He wants to keep his ass out of jail, and his son's ass safe from Hanes. You got something in mind?" asked the DA.

"Actually, I do. What do you all think about having St. James here introduced to the governor? He seems to be the type the governor likes, and we would have a slam-dunk conviction if he keeps to his MO."

"Does that mean we let St. James get snuffed out to make it a really tight case?" asked the chief.

With that, everyone laughed. They agreed to meet later in the day to present a plan using St. James as bait. Everyone seemed comfortable with the potential plan. Everyone but St. James. As they left the police station, St. James and Capstone got into Pat's cruiser.

"Holy shit, here we go again!" Capstone exclaimed.

"No shit. And I'm the bait, once again. This is getting to be a habit with the department."

"Well, that's what you get for being so damned good-looking!" Hank replied with a laugh.

"I can't wait for the next meeting later on today. We both better get home and get some sleep. By the way, how are things going with Shawn?"

"Incredible," Hank replied. "I'm getting laid in spades, and I can't wait to do it again. Shawn is a fantastic guy, has a great body, and a good sense of humor. He just might be husband material, Pat."

"Good to hear, Hank. Now our coffee connection is secure!"

They both laughed and then they parted ways. It would be just another ten hours before everyone met once again. Dean was at work by now, and so there was nothing to keep Pat from getting any sleep.

As the clock hit 4:00, the room filled with the strike force members. Fresh coffee and doughnuts, supplied by the DA's office, were on a table. Everyone looked like they had just fallen out of bed and forgot to comb their hair; everyone but the police chief, who always looked sharp in her uniform.

"Okay, while some of you got some sleep, others of us have been working on the plan for the investigation. Here is what we've come up with for consideration. We have Dugan give us a copy of the governor's schedule for the next two weeks and make sure that St. James is present at one of the events. It will be up to Dugan to make sure the governor is interested and meets with St. James for a sexual liaison. St. James will be under close watch in a hotel room that we have set up with sound and video. It will have a connecting door to another room that Hanes will believe Dugan is waiting in. Instead, it will be full of cops. Any questions so far?" asked the DA.

"How is Dugan going to make sure the governor wants to meet with me? And what capacity will I be in when he notices me? Security guard?" St. James asked.

"That part will be up to Dugan. He needs to make sure that you two end up together in a hotel room. We can't use the security guard routine, as it might make Hanes suspicious. Suggestions, anyone?" asked the DA.

"Well, Pat looks young enough to be a college student, so why don't we make him one that winds up at a function? I suggest that Pat pose as a waiter that handles the governor's food if we have a luncheon or dinner on the schedule," suggested the chief.

"St. James, do you think you can pull this off? You'll have to do a bit of flirting and withstand a little more than grab-ass for us to get him," asked the Homicide chief.

"Let me remind you of what I had to do in the Milford case. That was a lot more than just grab-ass, and, as far as I'm concerned, more dangerous," Pat answered.

"Okay. The first step is to get the governor's schedule and see where our best opportunity lies. We should have it by morning. We need this to take place in Prince George's County to retain jurisdiction over the investigation. Also, the State Police are not to be told of what's going on. I'm sure they can be trusted, but one never knows how working for this guy may have changed their loyalties," ordered the DA.

The chief turned to Pat. "Okay, St. James. You and Hank here are off of patrol and assigned to community relations. In reality, you will be working on this strike force, and I want your involvement in the planning of how this thing will go down. Use whatever resources you need. Until this case is closed, you have no other duties. Any questions from either of you?"

"No, ma'am," replied both rookies in unison.

"Okay," said the DA. "That's it until we have the schedule, then we go all out. Let's meet back here at eleven in the morning. Chief, if you can put together a support plan for our bait here, I would appreciate it."

"Will do," replied the chief.

"St. James and Capstone, please remain behind," the chief added.

As the room emptied out, Pat poured himself another cup of coffee. Hank seemed too nervous to even drink.

"I just wanted to say that I am pleased that you two guys are willing to go the extra mile in this case. I know that after the last case, you both were intent on returning to normal police work; but that seems not to be your fate in life. Do either of you have any qualms about getting deep into this thing? Especially you, Pat?"

"Not really, Chief. I got into police work to take out the bad guys, and if the governor is really a murderer, then he is fair game. To be honest, I kinda like the aspect of investigations even more than patrol work, so I am quite pleased to be involved in something this big. It's not every day that a rookie can grab for the gold ring. I am even more comfortable knowing that Hank here will be my close-in backup. We trust each other implicitly."

"I have to pretty much say the same, Chief," said Hank. "I like working closely with Pat, and we make a good team. The Milford case gave us invaluable experience in a very unique type of criminal investigation, and it will help us a lot in this case," said Hank.

"I know that you two are close and, in fact, work adjoining sectors. Let me be frank with both of you, and I assure you this conversation goes no further than the three of us. It is my understanding through the grapevine that you both may be gay, which is why your work in the Milford case was so brilliant. Personally, I don't care if you are gay; it doesn't matter any more. In fact, I highly doubt that a straight officer could be as effective as you two are in pulling off the types of things that you have to do in these kinds of cases. It is time that police departments everywhere get over the personal sexual lives of their officers as long as the relationships are of an adult nature. My only concern is that you two are not personally involved with each other off the job. This could cloud your judgment and that would concern me."

Hank spoke before Pat could.

"Chief, there is nothing sexual going on between Pat and me, on or off the job. We are close friends; that's it. As for being gay, I can't speak for Pat, but I'm tired of worrying about this issue becoming public knowledge and getting me fired from a job I was born to do. I am gay, Chief, but it does not affect my job in any way."

"Well, I can't very well let Hank here show me up by being ballsy. Yeah, I'm gay too, Chief. But on this job, as you know, some of the guys would not take kindly to this and, in fact, might endanger our lives on the street. This is why I am hoping that Hank and I can work closely, so that we have backup that we can count on."

"Well, first of all, thank you for being honest and trusting me. I also know that you are not the only gay cops in this department. Out of a department that is six hundred and twenty officers strong, there are more than likely at least sixty-two officers who are gay. Personally I have no issues with it at all as long as it has no impact on your performance. In fact, my sixteen-year-old son has told me he is gay, which took me a while to digest and accept. But I have, and it has caused me to become all the more sensitive to the issue. I also understand your concern about things like backup. It is a fact that we have to deal with. Some officers will always be antigay and there is nothing much we can do about it. But if I ever hear of someone not responding to a call for assistance because they think the other guy or gal is gay, then they are through being a cop. As for you two, as long as I am chief, you will always have each other for backup. That all being said, I want to add that I do not expect you, Pat, to go any further than a straight officer would in this investigation. In fact, as you well know, any sexual contact will jeopardize the case, as well as totally out you."

"Thanks, Chief, for your support. Hank and I appreciate it very much, and it is a relief to know that we are secure in our jobs on this issue. I am personally glad to hear that Hank and I will be working closely together for the foreseeable future. As for the investigation, I will not cross the line that separates proper and improper conduct. That would be the same as an undercover officer going into a massage parlor, and making the bust after he got the 'happy ending'. The public outcry would be loud, I'm sure."

"I agree totally with Pat on this, Chief. I am also glad to have this out so that it can be put behind us and allow us to concentrate only on the case, and not on any fears of losing our jobs."

"Great. Let's get moving on this case as quickly as possible. As soon as the plan of investigation is agreed on, we go full throttle until we have an arrest or indictment. As of now, you both are plainclothes until further notice," the chief said. "By the way, this case will be very good for both of your careers, and may lead to a gold shield."

"Well, that's always good to hear, Chief," Pat said with a smile.

"Okay, both of you take tomorrow and tomorrow night off, and report for duty the next morning. Once this thing gets rolling, I don't know when your next day off will be. I want you both rested and on your toes. Any questions?"

"No, ma'am," both of them answered in unison.

With that the meeting ended, and Hank and Pat left the stationhouse. They both felt great relief knowing that their secret was now known to the chief, and that they had nothing to worry about. This knowledge put a little extra spring in their step as they headed to their cars.

Chapter Twelve
Secrets

PAT had just finished cooking dinner when Dean came through the door. He looked a little tired, but his face lit up with a broad smile upon seeing Pat.

"Gimme a kiss, you big stud," Dean said.

"With pleasure, my love."

As they held each other, a feeling of peace and contentment fell upon Pat, and Dean appeared to have the same reaction. They were both in the arms of the man they loved. It couldn't get any better than that.

"You look a little tired tonight, honey. Everything okay?" Pat asked.

"Yeah. It was just one of those days where if something could go wrong, it did. I'm glad to be home. Whatever you're cooking smells great!"

"Well, it's ready, so get changed, and come to the table."

AFTER dinner, they both went into the living room. Dean made both of them a drink. He handed Pat his drink and smiled, knowing that even though he was tired, he could always go for a romp in the hay if he wanted to.

"So how was your day, Pat?"

"Good. Hank and I came out to the chief today and she took it like a champ. We have nothing to worry about; that was made plain."

"Why on earth would you do that? Didn't you both take a terrible chance with your jobs?"

"Well, it kinda came naturally as the result of an investigation Hank and I are going to be involved with shortly. Frankly, I am just as glad it did come up, since we now know she won't support any kind of termination should it become widely known we are gay."

"Oh God, what kind of investigation are you getting into now that would have your sexuality come up?"

"I really can't talk about this one, babe. I hope you understand. It's not that I don't trust you; it's that we have specific orders not to discuss this case with anyone. I can tell you it's big and will result in a ton of press."

"It's not the Milford bunch again, I hope?"

"No, nothing like that. It's just a murder case, but I can't say anything more, Dean."

"Okay, I understand. But just be careful. Don't they have any other cops that can do these investigations? Why you again?"

"It's because they don't have any other cops who are as cute as me or as hung as me!"

Dean laughed out loud and said, "Well, why don't we go to bed and see how hung you are?"

With that, Dean took his hand and they went up to their bedroom. Their relationship had progressed to the point where they no longer had sex – they made love.

The next day Pat called Hank just to talk, as he was getting a little nervous. It always helped to talk about an assignment like this so that it could be examined from many different angles.

"Hank? Pat. I'm a little uptight today. How about you?"

"Well, maybe a bit. After all, considering who the target is, this is national news stuff. We just need to try and relax today so that we are ready tomorrow. The captain called me earlier and told me we both need to report at eleven a.m. tomorrow. We'll be reporting that time each morning until the operation is over."

"Okay, that all sounds good. Hey, you wanna do something tonight, in the way of fun instead of talking about police work?" he asked.

"Hell, yeah. What do you have in mind?"

"Well, how about calling up that stud boyfriend of yours, and the four of us doing something?"

"Pat, do you remember what happened last time the four of us got together and did something? We became the targets of blackmail!"

"Yeah, well, look how that ended for the blackmailer. Okay, so gay bars are out, for tonight at least. How about dinner and a movie? Maybe we can all do something over a weekend break that is more interesting and fun."

"Yeah, that will work; nice and safe," Hank responded with a laugh.

"Okay, I'll call Dean at work and make sure he isn't having the day from hell at the bank, and we can meet around six for dinner. How's that sound?

"Works for me. I'll call Shawn now. We'll swing by in his car and pick you guys up. Be ready when I get there!"

The evening went fine and everyone had a great time. If Pat was honest with himself, he would have to admit that he was highly attracted to Shawn. After all, what's not to like in a guy that looked like he walked out of a catalog? He caught himself staring at Shawn a couple of times, remembering what Shawn looked like naked, not to mention what he tasted like, and he was sure that Shawn noticed. But Shawn was his usual easygoing self, and just smiled back at Pat. Shawn was used to gay men staring at him because his good looks clicked with a lot of men. The evening ended with Hank kissing Dean goodnight, and with Pat kissing Shawn goodnight. Hank and Pat just punched each other on the arm and promised to be fully rested for the next day's events.

"That was fun tonight, Pat. I'm glad you set that up," Dean observed in the quiet of their bedroom.

"Yeah, it was. Shawn and Hank seem to be getting along real well, and I couldn't be happier about it. He needs someone in his personal life that he can find love with, which some cops never find."

"Well, then maybe you shouldn't cruise Shawn quite so openly, huh? It might hurt Hank's feelings, don'tcha think?"

"What? You have to be kidding. I never cruised Shawn! Where did you get that idea?"

"Well, the two times I noticed it, your eyes were almost transfixed on Shawn's basket. Not that I blame you; he was *wearing* those jeans!"

"I never did any such thing! Well, maybe once I might have glanced down, but that's all."

"Glanced down? If your eyes were magnifying glasses and the sun was out, you would have set Shawn's crotch on fire! Don't worry; I'm not mad. I kinda like him too. But, you were rather indiscreet with your eyes, and I wouldn't want you to hurt your friend, Hank," Dean said, with some concern.

"Okay, okay, maybe I did check him out. I can't help it; he is one hot young man. I don't think Shawn minded at all. In fact, at one point, he spread his legs so I could get a better look."

"Well, as long as look is all you do, I don't mind. Just be careful not to piss off Hank."

"Let's go to bed and end this conversation. I can't help it that I find pretty boys a turn-on. After all, that's what attracted me to you!" Pat said with a laugh.

Chapter Thirteen
Feeling the Sting

It was now Thursday morning and it had been two days since the first major meeting of the task force. As Hank and Pat headed into the station, Hank said, "I wonder if the governor's schedule has been delivered to the detective bureau yet? That schedule, Pat, could quite possibly contain the key to the arrest and conviction of the governor of the state of Maryland and our rise in the department."

"I know. It really is odd how fate plays into one's hands at times like these."

They had arrived a few minutes early for the meeting, grabbed a cup of coffee, and began to read the morning newspaper. One by one, the rest of the team entered the conference room, the noise level rising with each addition. The chief entered the room, greeted everyone, and almost at once was on the phone dealing with some administrative issue that had come up earlier in the morning. When the DA arrived, things began to settle down and the meeting began.

"Good morning, everyone. I hope you are all well-rested. We received the fax an hour ago from our informant and we now have the target's schedule for the next three weeks. He has a couple of meetings scheduled here in the county, but nothing in those that would give us any opportunities. However, thanks to the nature of politics, he does have one fund-raising dinner scheduled at the Hilton once again. Next Thursday night, he will arrive at the Hilton around six in the evening with a predicted departure of ten a.m. the next morning. The governor is actually spending the night at the hotel! The dinner is for high-dollar contributors only, and will set these loyal supporters back two thousand dollars a plate. This is our opportunity to introduce our undercover officer to the governor and see what happens."

The DA looked at the Chief of Detectives and asked, "Can you contact the people at the Hilton and get St. James and Capstone positions that will bring them into contact with the governor?"

Captain Anderson replied, "Yes, sir. We'll use the excuse that we want cops close to the governor because of a threat that we received. We'll tell them that the governor doesn't like a lot of police present around him at these fund-raisers because he feels it will insinuate that he travels in fear of being hurt. This way we can insist that no one in the governor's party be told that our guys are undercover at the function, including the State Police detail."

"Where are we going to put our guys?" the chief asked.

"I suggest in the position of waiters that serve the head table. I'll make sure that the governor notices me," interjected Pat.

"Okay, that sounds like it would work. Captain Anderson, can you pull that off?" asked the DA.

"Should be no problem. Do you have any waiter experience, St. James? After all, we don't want you dumping a bowl of hot soup into the governor's lap," Anderson commented.

"I waited on tables back in college like most other guys did," he answered.

"And I worked as a busboy in my teens," added Hank.

"Great. That should work out nicely," the DA said.

"I'll pay the Hilton a visit after this meeting and set it up. I'll also talk to the security chief over there and get a couple of connecting rooms put aside for us to use. The guy is retired PG County Police so I know we can count on his cooperation," said Anderson.

"I want St. James wired so that we can hear and record every word that takes place between the Governor and him. In fact, wire both him and Capstone in case the governor's taste runs towards Capstone instead," ordered the DA.

"Okay, that's no problem," replied Anderson.

"This guy is a murderer and a slime ball. We want him nailed good. No fuckups. Everyone understand?" asked the DA.

Everyone nodded and the meeting was adjourned.

Final preparations for the operation were made, with the Hilton cooperating fully. When the governor stayed at the Hilton, he was always given the "Governor's Suite." This was a suite on the seventh floor of the hotel that was accessed by a special key card via the elevator. Adjacent to the suite were additional rooms on each side with connecting doors for security personnel and guests. When all the inner doors were opened, it could become a three-bedroom suite. The suite included a dining room, living room, wet bar, and two marble bathrooms. The connecting rooms were a little more opulent than regular hotel rooms, but nothing compared to the suite.

The State Police always took one of the connecting rooms and Bill Dugan usually took the other. This time, however, one connecting room would house the surveillance equipment as well as part of the strike force necessary to record the events and protect the undercover officers. The lock on the governor's side would be disabled to ensure that the team could get into the suite without delay.

Hotel security met with the captain and the department's technicians and wired the suite for sound and video. The department was fortunate enough to have the funds to buy the very latest surveillance equipment, which meant that the equipment was also the small, high-tech, easily concealed variety, which made the job even easier. All that was left to be done was to wait for the calendar to change to the date for the fund-raising dinner. To the team, it seemed like an eternity. Especially to Patrick St. James.

AT the governor's office, all was not peaceful and serene. The daily exchange between the governor and his chief of staff had become more of a bullfighting session; the normal work atmosphere that had existed in the past was gone.

"Bill, I asked you to have your son in here last Monday so that he could begin to learn his position in this administration and get a taste for the politics of life and government. This is Tuesday of the following week, and he still has not reported for work. You say he is sick. Well, he must need to be hospitalized by now if he is still as sick as you indicated to me last week."

"Governor, he has a bad flu bug that just will not let go of him. He isn't avoiding coming to work. After all, this is a dream job for him. But he has to get well, and I don't want him infecting the office with this virus. Do you?"

"No, of course not. I'm just, well, disappointed that he hasn't been around the office here learning his trade. I'll tell you what: Why don't I have the Capitol doctor go over to your house and take a look at him and maybe speed up his recovery. What do you say?"

"Thank you, Governor. That really is kind of you, but he has been seen by his own doctor, and we are following his advice and taking care of the situation. I guarantee you that he will be ready for anything here in the office in another two weeks. No question of that."

"Two weeks, huh? Well, in two weeks, you can announce your run for office and begin your campaign. That's the deal. When he comes in to fill some of your duties like scheduling, then I can afford to have you go off on the campaign trail."

"Sure, that's no problem, Governor. After all, we don't want you shortchanged from what you deserve staff-wise. I'm sure my son can't wait to begin his work for you."

With that Bill got up and left the office. He knew that he had left a smiling governor behind.

Fuck you, asshole. You're going to get what you deserve, but it won't be ass. It will be an orange jumpsuit and bars, he thought.

As he entered his office area, his secretary greeted him and announced that the Hilton hotel's general manager in Prince George's County was on the phone for him.

"Should I take a message or pass the call to logistics?" she asked.

"No, thank you. I will take the call."

He wondered what the Hilton wanted and he started to get a case of nerves.

"Mr. Dugan, George Thompson here. I'm the new general manager of the Hilton in Prince George's County."

"Yes, Mr. Thompson. What can I do for you?"

"Why, I just wanted to let you know that things are coming along fine for the governor's visit next week. The PG County Police have been here, and we have made a couple of changes to the usual things that the governor likes in order to comply with their requests."

"Changes? What changes are you referring to, Mr. Thompson?"

"Well, we were happy to allow the two police officers to function as waiters for the governor without the governor knowing about it, and we have permitted the police to install extra security devices in the governor's room. Was there anything else we can do for you or the governor?"

He was completely stunned that the general manager of the hotel where the governor was being set up was now on the phone revealing details that surely would have tipped off the governor had the call been given to anyone else. What the hell was going on?

"Why, thank you, Mr. Thompson. There is one other thing you can do for me and the governor."

"Of course. What is it?"

"Never mention these things again to anyone, including the governor. They are security matters that must receive the utmost secrecy, and that occurs by not speaking about them. Do you understand, Mr. Thompson?"

"Ah, yes, I do. Did I say something wrong, sir?" asked the now timid hotel manager.

"No, no. It's just that we never talk about these things as a matter of security, especially on the telephone. So, other than just keeping quiet, there is nothing further you need to do, Mr. Thompson."

"Ah, I see. No problem. You can count on us here at the Hilton to make sure everything is perfect. Please call me if I can do anything else."

"Thank you, Mr. Thompson."

He hung up the phone and shook his head. If his secretary had given that call to logistics or the security detail, the plan would have been blown. Why hadn't the cops told this guy to shut the hell up?

He pulled up the private number for the DA in Prince George's County and dialed the number.

"Hello. Mike Jenkins, please, Bill Dugan calling."

A few seconds later, Mike's voice greeted him.

"Mike, this is Bill Dugan. I just had a phone call that has unnerved me a bit."

"Oh? From who and about what?"

"The general manager of the Hilton in PG County. A Mr. Thompson called me a few minutes ago, and took great pains to assure me that he has gone along with all of the 'special arrangements' that have been made for the governor, including the use of undercover police officers to wait on the governor."

"What? You have got to be fucking kidding me. Who else has he spoken to, do you know?"

"Apparently, I'm the only one, but my secretary almost gave the call to logistics, which would have derailed this thing but good. I told him to mention this stuff to no one else and I made sure he understood."

"Look, I'll have the cops have a chat with this guy to make sure he didn't talk to anyone else. It's always the little things that happen that you don't count on or didn't anticipate that ruin an otherwise great case. Have there been any changes to the schedule that we need to know about?"

"No, everything is the same. Please let me know ASAP if you find that this guy has spilled the beans, will you? I'll need to make sure my family is safe."

"No problem. I'll get back with you."

With that, Mike hung up the phone and dialed Chief of Detectives Anderson. Anderson was told what had happened, and was asked to send a couple of detectives to talk to the hotel manager and report back ASAP.

As Anderson was getting the phone call from the DA, both Hank and Pat were at the hotel filling out phony job applications so that they would be seen in there looking like college kids trying to find a job. Once the applications were submitted, the security chief would take the applications and issue the clearance for both of them to work in the food and beverage department. The director of banquets would be told by the general manager to put both of them on the head table the night of the dinner. This would finish the basic setup of the investigation. The rest would be up to Hank and Pat and, of course, the governor.

The detectives paid a quick visit to the general manager and confirmed that he had relayed details of the special arrangements to no one other than the governor's chief of staff. Satisfied that their operation had not been compromised, it went forward as planned.

IT was still another three nights until the big night at the Hilton, and Pat needed to relax and have some fun. He decided that he and Dean needed to have a get-together with Hank and Shawn; after all, the weekend had arrived.

"Honey, I want to have some fun tonight. Let's get together with Hank and Shawn, okay?"

Dean turned around and smiled at his mate, and asked, "You really are fond of Hank, aren't you?"

"Yeah, I like him a lot. 'Course, it doesn't hurt that our lives depend on each other when we are at work, but it's more than that. I genuinely like him. As for Shawn, what's not to like? Woof!"

Dean tackled his horny lover onto the sofa and pretended that he was all upset at the "woof."

"I'll give you woof!" Dean said.

"Promises, promises. Words are cheap, actions speak louder!"

"Yeah, well, not now. I have a headache," Dean replied while cracking up.

"Fine. I'm going to call my other 'boyfriends' and see if they are up for doing something tonight. I know Hank has this stupid thing about not liking to go to the movies on a Friday or Saturday night, but he'll just have to get over that crap."

Pat dialed the phone.

"Hank? Pat. Do you want to do something tonight?"

"Yeah, I don't want to sit around the apartment here. What do you have in mind?"

"Something simple. Why don't we just go get some ice cream and walk around at the mall?"

"Okay. Sounds fine. Shawn is here so we'll be over in an hour," said Hank.

The night passed peacefully and all had a good time, as usual.

Chapter Fourteen
Cake or Cock

THE day of the sting operation had arrived and all parties were tense with anticipation. A major law enforcement case that would inevitably make media stars out of the principle police players was about to commence. As the strike team began to arrive at the station, the technical team was already at the Hilton hotel double-checking the surveillance equipment in the governor's suite. As planned, the one adjoining room was set up to operate as the command center where the events would unfold and be recorded.

The meeting was called to order at noon.

"Okay. Everyone settle down please and let's get started; we have a lot to cover," said the DA.

As the room came to order, a quiet anticipatory mood clearly showed upon the faces of the principles present. Everyone was well aware of the enormity of the events about to come to fruition. No one, however, was more tense and, at the same time, confident, than Patrick St. James. He knew that the success of the sting fell squarely upon his shoulders, for if he did not pull off his part, there would be no arrest or indictment. Pat had to make sure that the case against the governor was airtight.

"Okay. We just heard from the police tech unit and the hotel rooms are wired for picture and sound, and everything has checked out okay. We have also received a phone call from the governor's chief of staff, and the schedule is on track. We should expect the suspect here in our fair county sometime early this evening. St. James and Capstone are set to go undercover posing as waiters, with backup near them both at all times," the DA recapped.

"What time do Capstone and I have to report to the hotel so that everything looks normal to the other employees?" Pat asked.

"The regular policy is that you are there by three-thirty to assist with the setup in the ballroom. You begin the food service part around six-thirty after opening remarks by the governor. You and Capstone are assigned to the head table," answered Anderson, the Chief of Detectives.

"St. James, how exactly do you propose to entice the governor into hitting on you?" asked the chief.

"Most of it is going to be played by ear. I'll start out by smiling at the governor and standing close to him while I serve the food and drinks. This will give him a chance to either talk to me, or at least touch me to indicate any interest that he might have in me. If he ignores me, we'll move Capstone into the same position and see if that works," he answered.

"Do not, I repeat, do not come on to the governor. Let him make all the moves. I do not want the issue of entrapment to come up at trial," said the DA.

"Understood, sir," Pat replied as Hank nodded his head in agreement.

"You are to report to a Denise Johnson when you get to the hotel. She works in Banquets and will be the one to give you your orders on the floor. If the governor makes his move, we will hear it on the wire. It is vital that you get invited up to his suite for any action that he has in mind. Don't let him get you in a men's room or anything like that. We need all this on tape; both video and audio. Your backup will be in the next room. We don't want you to end up on a slab at the morgue," continued the detective chief.

"Chief, everything else in place?" asked the DA.

"Yes. We have two officers, one of them being Sergeant Durkin, assigned to the adjoining room, three officers on the floor of the banquet room, the surveillance technicians, you, Mr. DA., and finally me. I want to be present to make sure nothing goes wrong," the police chief answered.

"Then all we need is the governor to play his part, and we have a sting in progress!" said the DA.

"Okay, let's move this sting to the operations center and all principles to the hotel. Everyone stay on their toes," said the chief.

As the operations center became alive with activity, Hank and Pat got into Pat's private vehicle and headed to the hotel. They wanted to make sure that everything was in place and ready for this evening. When they pulled into the employee area of the parking lot, they both put their service weapons into the glove box, leaving just Hank with a two-inch .38 in an ankle holster.

"Well, let's get this show on the road," Pat said to Hank as they exited the vehicle.

They entered the hotel and went to the banquet room, where some employees were already setting up tables and chairs. The head table was set up on a riser in order for everyone to see the VIPs in attendance.

"Are you the two new guys for the banquet tonight?" asked a nice-looking blonde woman as she walked toward the undercover officers.

"Yes. I'm Pat, and this is Hank."

"Okay. Glad you are both here, but I gotta be honest with you. Having never worked with you before I'm nervous having you guys waiting on the governor's party tonight. But that decision was made over my head, so if you screw up, it's not my neck."

"We understand, but you can relax. We are both experienced and will have no problems. If something comes up that we don't know how to handle, we will locate you and ask, okay?" Pat replied.

"Good enough. For now, set the head table with the dinnerware and put the flowers out as well. Make sure the flowers have water in them. I don't want them sitting down to wilted arrangements." With that the banquet supervisor turned and walked away. As she passed one of the waitresses, she said something to her and pointed over to Pat and Hank.

"Hi, guys. I'm Charlene, and I'm supposed to show you where everything is, so let's hit the kitchen. We only have another two hours to get everything set up."

As Hank and Pat started their roles as waiters, they knew that plainclothes police were making their way up to room 709, which was adjacent to the governor's suite. Room 715 was also filling up with extra backup officers if needed. As the chief of police entered the room, she quickly went into the governor's suite to check and make sure none of the surveillance equipment was visible. The suite was impressive. Fresh flowers adorned the dining table and were also placed at various locations around the rooms, and a fully stocked wet bar stood ready to serve its guests.

The chief went back into the adjacent room and shut the door so that it could not be opened from the other side.

"Okay, everyone stay out of the governor's suite from now on. Everything looks good in there and, unless an urgent need arises, we need to stay out of there. The hotel will vacuum the room shortly for a final time, which will erase our footsteps in the carpet," the chief said.

After looking at his watch, the chief of detectives announced that the advance team of state troopers would arrive in about an hour, to make sure everything was secure. All noise had to cease at that point in order not to alert the troopers that someone was in the adjoining room. The hotel would tell them that a diplomat from the Middle East was registered in the room and that it was, for all legal purposes, a foreign mission. This would prevent anyone from entering the room without the diplomat's permission.

"We have arranged with the superintendent of the Maryland State Police to provide us with this little device that will tell us where the governor's limo is at all times. His car has a tracking chip embedded into the frame of the car and we'll know when he gets close to the hotel. The chip was put there in case the governor is ever kidnapped," said the detective chief. "Now we want to know where he is for a very different reason."

In the main banquet room, the tables were set, and place cards were put out on the tables. It was a very rich and important cross-segment of society that would soon fill up the room. A final inspection of the head table was finished by the supervisor and, with a few adjustments, it too was also ready.

"Okay, can I have everyone's attention please? It's now four-fifty. and we have just a little over an hour before the guest of honor arrives, which means that the other guests will start to arrive in probably another forty minutes. Fill the glasses with ice water and make sure each table has the first course ready to be served," said the supervisor.

As the banquet manager finished giving her orders in the banquet room, a beep let everyone in the hotel command post know that the governor's limo was in motion. The indication on the GPS system was that the limo was leaving the state capitol, Annapolis, and heading toward Prince George's County.

"Well, all the players are in motion now," observed the DA. "I can't think of anything we've missed, so it's all up to St. James now."

The hotel security director notified the command post that the advance police team had just arrived and he would be meeting them momentarily. The first thing they wanted to do was to see the banquet room, and then head straight to the governor's suite. After a lengthy explanation as to why they did not have access to the one adjoining room, the detail was satisfied that everything was normal. They alerted the escort vehicle by radio that it was okay to proceed to the hotel location.

"Okay, according to our little friend here, the target is now about fifteen minutes from the hotel. There is no way they are doing the speed limit to be this close already," said the detective chief.

"Who's going to give them a ticket?" someone in the room mumbled.

"Time to turn on the body mics on St. James and Capstone and start recording whatever comes in range," ordered the DA.

Both mics were working perfectly and the occupants of the room quietly listened to casual banter between a waitress who was hitting on St. James and his responses to her. The supervisor interrupted their conversation much to St. James' relief, with the announcement that the governor and his party would be there at any moment, and that all wait staff should take their places.

The banquet room had already filled up with invited guests and the level of noise rose exponentially. Pat and Hank had taken their places behind the head table, each with a waiter's towel over his left arm. All was in place and ready for the main event.

In the seventh floor command post, it was announced that the limo was arriving on the hotel's block as indicated by the tracking device. As the technicians made sure all cameras were now recording, the governor and his chief of staff stepped out of the limo and walked into the front door of the hotel. The governor made his usual grand entrance. Normally, government officials were driven into the underground garage and came up in a private elevator to their destination in a much more secure fashion. But not this governor. He loved the publicity and attention.

The general manager of the hotel along with the security director met the governor in the lobby and welcomed him to the Hilton. He then escorted the governor's party into the side entrance of the banquet room where he entered to the sound of applause from the assembled crowd. The governor smiled and waved to the attendees, already in reelection campaign mode, as he strode toward the head table. Pat stepped forward and pulled the governor's chair out for him, making sure that Hanes got a look at him. Hank did the same thing for the chief of staff, who looked as frightened as an eighteen-year-old virgin on his first visit to a leather bar.

"Thank you, son," said the governor to Pat in response to his gesture.

Pat noticed that the governor's eyes glanced down at the package that Pat was showing in his purposely-altered tight pants.

"If there is anything I can get you, Governor, just ask," he said.

The governor just smiled without answering. Once he was seated, the salad course began to arrive from the kitchen and was served to the various tables. Pat and Hank went over to the waiter who brought out the salads and took them from him to serve the head table. As Pat and the waiter looked at each other, they realized they knew each other. The other waiter quickly remembered where he'd seen Pat before.

"You're a cop! What are you doing here serving a banquet?"

"Shut your mouth now, and get back into the fucking kitchen!" ordered Pat. Hank grabbed one arm, and Pat the other and together they whisked the kid through the doors back into the prep kitchen.

The command post heard the conversation and quickly radioed two detectives to take custody of the waiter and remove him from the property ASAP.

"What the fuck are you doing? I didn't do anything wrong!" yelled the kid.

As he said that, Pat realized that he was one of the college guys who had gotten into the bar fight in College Park and was arrested with nine other guys for being drunk and disorderly.

"Shut your mouth now, or I'll charge you with impeding a police investigation. You understand?"

Before the kid could answer, the detectives arrived and removed him from the hotel via the back door of the kitchen area. They put him into a waiting unmarked police cruiser.

"Damn, that could have been a major hemorrhoid had he done that within ear shot of the governor or his people," said Hank.

"Okay. Situation contained, returning to the floor," he said into his mic so that the seventh floor knew the sting was back on track.

"Okay, Hank. You put the salad in front of him so that he gets a good look at you also."

"Right."

The chief of staff talked nervously to his table companions while occasionally glancing at the governor. In some respects, he couldn't wait for the governor to be arrested. However, he dreaded the publicity and court cases that were to follow. His career in politics was over and he had no idea where to go for a job after this all came out, assuming he stayed out of jail.

The salad course was taken away, and the main course was ready to be served. Pat dropped a fork on the floor next to the target, hoping the governor would once again check him out. He wasn't disappointed.

"I'm always doing that at my house. I just get clumsy when handling silverware. Is it the same with you, young man?"

"I'm afraid so, sir, but I hope not to be dropping things by the time I leave this job."

"What do you want to do when you leave?"

"Well, I am majoring in political science at the University of Maryland, so I hope to be involved in politics after graduation," Pat answered, baiting the hook.

"Really? What year are you in at school?"

"I'm a senior, Governor, and just working to help pay the bills at this point. Hopefully, I can land something decent soon after graduation."

"Well, I'll tell you what. Why don't we talk about your future after this banquet is over? I'm staying here at the hotel and we could have a chat about it. I might be able to help you with an internship."

Pat feigned shock and replied, "Wow, Governor that would be great if you would help me out."

"Fine. Come up to my suite, the governor's suite, around eleven. How's that sound?"

"Great, sir. And thank you very much. I would be most grateful for your assistance."

With that the governor smiled and ran his hand over Pat's ass.

As he turned around and walked over to the water pitchers, he mumbled into his mic, "The bastard just felt up my ass."

The chief of staff had noticed the sexual contact and just hung his head. How sad that he had hooked up his wagon to a maniac.

In the seventh floor command post, everyone was all smiles.

"Well, if he not only invited St. James to the room, but also patted him on the ass, I think we got ourselves a successful operation unfolding," said the DA.

The chief agreed and was silently grateful for the fact that St. James was willing to deal with these touchy situations. She knew that only a few cops would have let themselves be touched in that manner in the line of duty. But with the apparent success of this sting, the chief started to tense up even more. She knew what kind of media circus was going to explode over this arrest.

On the banquet floor, Pat motioned for Hank to come over to him.

"I've been invited back to his room, and he had the nerve to slide his hand down over my ass while he was at it."

"No shit. Those pants really worked! We got him; we are actually going to pull this off. I've got a suggestion. Tell him that I'm looking for a job too and ask if you should ask me if I would like to join you."

"No, that won't work. If there are two of us, he won't try anything violent, and violence is part of this guy's sexual genus. Just go up to the command post when you split from here and be ready to get to me if I need it."

"Okay, you got it."

As the main course was cleared away and coffee and desert was served, it was time for the mandatory speeches from the head table. First up was the chairman of the State Republican Party, who thanked everyone for coming to the dinner. He then spent ten minutes trying to explain all of the governor's accomplishments for the state, and why he deserved another term in office. Finally, he made the introduction, and the governor gave his speech.

As the governor droned on, Pat could feel his stomach begin to tighten. It was the same feeling he had during the murder investigation that led him to the religious-nut clan that was killing gays.

When the governor finished his speech, he sat down. As the applause died down, he leaned over to the chief of staff and said, "I have an appointment at eleven, so don't disturb me. If I need you for anything, I will call your room, understand?"

"Yes, Governor," Bill replied meekly.

"And tell the security detail that they can knock off for the night once I'm in the room."

"Yes, sir."

It was 10:40 when the speeches were over and the governor worked his way through the guests, shaking hands. He headed to the elevator followed by the state police. He said goodnight to the troopers at the door to his suite and entered by himself. Closing the door, he removed his jacket and tie, and poured himself a drink from the wet bar in the suite.

The governor was excited at the prospect of getting his hands on the waiter with the great ass. He had sensed vulnerability in the young man and a thirst for success. That was the weakness in all of these "pretty-boy" types. Well, he would give him a job all right, and it wasn't the one he was expecting. The governor felt himself getting hard at the thought of fucking the waiter.

The only problem that bothered him was how to kill the boy and get rid of the body. Then it occurred to him; he would simply follow his usual plan and inject the waiter so that it looked like the waiter was a junkie and had merely overdosed. Once the deed was done, he would open the door to the adjoining room that held his security detail and plead for help, saying that the waiter had come to his room and attempted to assault him. He knew he wasn't popular in all quarters of the state, so it would be plausible that he could be assaulted because of his policies. Opening his brief case, he took out the drugs, hypodermic needle, lube and condoms and put them on a tray from the bar. Then he shoved the tray underneath the sofa where his victim would be sitting, unable to fight off the impending rape.

Pat and Hank were preparing to leave the banquet room and go to the seventh floor. As they took off their waiter jackets, the supervisor approached them.

"Where do you two think you're going? We have a couple of hours' worth of work here in cleanup."

"Sorry, Denise, but we both have to go. We have prior commitments," responded Hank.

"Prior commitments? Are you serious? This is your job! If you leave, you are both fired."

"Well, it's been a real pleasure to work here at the Hilton, and we thank you for being so understanding. We're going," he said as a look of anger fell across the supervisor's face.

"College kids! Useless!" yelled the supervisor at the back of their heads as they left the room.

"Okay, everyone; it's almost time for act two of this little drama to begin. Everyone wake up and pay attention," said the DA. "And for God's sake, turn down all radios and no talking. We don't want any noise going through the door or a wall and letting him know this room has someone in it."

Hank quietly knocked on the door to the surveillance room and gained access. Once inside, he was grilled about any details that did not come over the mics both he and Pat wore.

Chapter Fifteen
Foreplay

AT precisely 11:00, Pat knocked on the governor's door and waited. Inside the room, the governor swallowed his drink. He got up to answer the door, but only after he knocked again. That was part of the game: Let them wait a bit to increase the victim's anxiety.

"Come in, young man, and make yourself comfortable. Would you like a drink?"

"Just a soda if you have any here, Governor. Wow, I can't believe that I'm talking to the Governor of Maryland in his hotel suite. The guys will never believe it!" he said, laying on the innocent act.

"Well, I like to encourage youths to get ahead in this world, and to strive for things that make their dreams come true," Hanes replied while handing Pat a soda laced with 40 milligrams of liquid valium.

"Well, I can't tell you how much I appreciate your asking to see me tonight. I'm sure you are tired and want to get to sleep, so I won't stay long."

"Actually, I took a nap this afternoon so that I could stay up with no problems this evening, so we can talk as long as we like."

"I've got to ask, Governor, do you usually go out of your way to help guys like me? I mean, I don't know how I could ever repay your kindness. Getting the assistance of a state's governor is no small matter."

"Well, maybe you can show me your appreciation in some way. We'll see."

Pat began to feel the effects of the mickey he was drinking, and realized that he was being drugged through the soda. *You son of a bitch,* he thought to himself after realizing what was going on. He decided to act like the drug was having a more pronounced effect on him than it actually was to make the governor make his move sooner rather than later.

As Pat yawned, he said, "Oh, forgive me. I guess it's been a long day and a long evening and I feel kinda tired all of a sudden."

"Well, just relax then, put your head back and rest for a moment. While you're doing that, I'm gonna change into something other than this suit. It's been a long day for both of us."

When the governor left the room to enter the suite's bedroom, Pat gave a signal toward one of the hidden cameras in the room in an attempt to let his fellow officers know what was happening. He picked up the soda, and made the motion of pouring something into it, and then putting his head to the side with his hands together in the universally recognized symbol for sleep. Pat then poured most of the soda into one of the flower arrangements so that it appeared that he had drank more than he had.

IT worked. The strike force immediately picked up on the signal and realized that Pat had been drugged.

"That bastard!" Hank whispered.

The chief picked up her cell phone, went into the bathroom, and called the county police dispatch office.

"Nine-one-one. What's your emergency?"

"This is Chief Morgan. Have an ambulance crew with paramedics on board standing by two blocks from our present location, and no sirens. I want them to remain there until released by me personally. We may need them in a hurry here at the hotel. Understand?"

"Yes, Chief. We'll set that in motion at once."

The chief hung up and returned to watching the TV screens.

By the time the governor returned to the living room where Pat was, the officer was feeling no pain. His eyes were slightly droopy and he wanted to sleep.

"So, how you doing, guy?" asked the governor.

"Well, I'm kinda sleepy from being on my feet all day. I apologize for not being more active. Maybe we should talk some other time, if you are still interested in talking with me."

"Tell you what, why don't you spend the night here in the suite and go home in the morning. That way I don't have to worry about you falling asleep at the wheel and killing yourself or someone else. Then in the morning, we can have breakfast together and you can scoot afterwards before the rest of the world wakes up. What do you say?"

"That's really nice of you, Governor, but maybe I can get a hotel room on the house and that way I won't interfere with your privacy and routine."

"No, I wouldn't hear of it. Please, stay and be my guest. You can shower up and then we can get to sleep. If you don't mind, we can share the king-size bed in the bedroom. Plenty of room in that thing. Why, I bet we could throw a party in that bed!"

Pat knew the governor was setting up the trap, and he went along.

"Okay. You win, Governor. I'll shower now before I fall asleep. Would you mind pouring me another soda while I'm in the shower?"

"Of course!" the governor responded as his private cell phone began to ring.

Pat went into the bathroom and left the door slightly ajar so that the governor would be able to get an eyeful if he so desired. He carefully removed the wire from his body and buried it in his clothing to keep it from being seen by the governor.

As he stood under the water, he suddenly began to giggle to himself in his present altered state of mind. He wondered if the tech guys had put a camera in the bathroom, and he found that possibility funny for some reason.

He turned off the water and stepped out from behind the curtains to find the governor standing there with a towel in his hands, looking down at Pat's cock.

"I thought I would bring you a towel so that you could dry off without walking over to the towel rack. Have you ever seen a bathroom so large in your life?"

"No. It is quite big, and with the marble floors a little cold. I'll take that towel now, thank you."

"Of course, here. My, but you have a fine body for a college student. Do you work out?"

"Well, as often as I can, but I need to work out more. I'm trying to build up my pecs."

"Well, your pecs look just fine to me, along with everything else."

Pat finished drying himself off and wrapped the towel around his hips. He looked around for the clothes that he took off before showering and could not find them. Walking out of the expansive bathroom, he saw that the Governor had kicked them into a corner and covered them with a towel.

"You know, sir, I was thinking that I should just sleep here on the sofa and let you have the bed all to yourself. I'm not used to sleeping with another man in my bed and don't know if I could get to sleep."

"Sit down and let's talk a bit. You want a job in my office when you graduate from college?"

"Well, that would be a fantastic opportunity for someone just getting out of college, so how could I turn it down?" he said while taking another sip of his newly drugged soda refill.

"Well, I'll help you out if you'll help me out. That sounds fair, doesn't it?"

Pat began to feel lightheaded and wondered if he would be able to stay awake. His only comfort was in knowing that a room full of cops was on the other side of the wall.

He responded in a slurred speech pattern. "What could I possibly do to help out a man like you?"

"How are you feeling, young man?"

"Actually, I feel weird. Like I'm gonna fall asleep and there is nothing I can do about it."

"Good. That's very good. What can you do for me? You can take off that towel and let me have your body. What do you say to that?"

"Huh? Did you just say that you want my body? You mean you want to have sex with me?"

"Well, more aptly put would be that I want to rape you, my young friend. I love taking the prize much more than when it is given up to me. Now just relax, and you won't even know when I stick my cock up your fucking ass."

Pat tried to get up but was unable to rise to his feet. He felt the governor come over to him and pull the towel off his body, and felt him shove him back onto the sofa. Pat's cock was exposed to his assailant's hungry eyes.

AS Hank watched in the command post, he asked, "Should we move in now?"

"Almost, but not quite yet. Stay calm and wait. St. James is a professional and knows how far this has to go to nail this bastard good," responded the DA, with the chief nodding in agreement. "The cameras are recording every moment of the complete self-destruction of the governor, and he is sealing his fate with the jury."

"That's it, boy. Just relax and it will all be over before you know it."

As he said that, the governor fondled his dick and balls. He knelt down as if he was going to blow Pat, but instead pulled out a small tray from under the sofa and put it on the coffee table. On the tray were lube, a rubber, and a syringe with two bottles of liquid.

"Son of a bitch! Where did that come from?" asked the Chief of Detectives.

"He hid it under the sofa when you were on the phone. We won't let him actually inject anything into Pat. Just get ready to move in now," ordered the DA.

The governor fondled Pat until Pat got an erection that was a natural response to his sexual organs being manually manipulated. Pat was borderline unconscious, but still remained awake enough to know what was going on. The governor swiftly went down on Pat's hard-on, and then quickly rolled him over onto the floor so that Pat's ass was pointing up.

As the witnesses in the surveillance room watched, they observed the governor begin his final moves.

"Now my boy, I'm gonna fuck you good, and it's probably your first time getting a dick up your ass, so I hope you are awake enough to feel the pleasure or the pain. I really don't care which."

"Almost. Hold on, everyone," the DA ordered the angry cops waiting to pounce on the criminal in the next room.

The governor now stripped off all his clothes in a rapid movement of his hands and quickly put a rubber on his dick and began to apply lube to Pat's asshole. Pat thought to himself, *Okay, guys: Any time now. This guy is really going to butt-fuck me!*

But as he was ready to begin the rape, Hanes stopped, turned, and filled a syringe with one of the liquids. He then reached over to Pat's pants, and pulled the belt out of the loops and placed it on the sofa.

"This, my young pretty friend, is for after your fucking. It will make sure you remember nothing at all, ever again. In fact, you will be dead."

Having said that, the governor began to inch closer to Pat's exposed ass to insert his cock.

The time had come.

"Now, get in there and arrest that bastard!" hissed the DA.

With the order having been given, the cops burst through the door and into the governor's suite. Hank led the charge and literally threw himself through the air, landing on the governor. He knocked him, the coffee table, and a chair over in the process. The deadly syringe went flying through the air and stuck into a wall.

The chief summoned the paramedics to move in and get up to the suite to administer any necessary medical treatment. Two officers covered Pat's nakedness with his towel and moved him up onto the sofa.

As that was happening, Hank was cuffing the shocked and bewildered Governor while at the same time reading him his Miranda rights. Because of all the shouting, the Maryland State Police security detail burst through the adjoining bedroom door in order to get to their charge. With guns drawn, the troopers yelled, "Freeze or we'll fire!"

The District Attorney showed his badge and yelled back at the troopers.

"The governor is under arrest and is to be prosecuted by my office for murder and numerous other crimes. Put away your weapons."

The chief spoke up. "I'm Chief Morgan of the Prince George's County Police. Do as he says. He'll explain it all to you, but the governor is under arrest and will be taken to Homicide for processing in Forestville."

The troopers were in a state of shock as they took in the entire scene. There was a naked young man with a towel over his lap, overturned furniture, cops, and the local district attorney. But the real breath-taker was the fact that the governor was also naked and on the floor in handcuffs. As the situation began to dawn on the troopers, they holstered their weapons and sat down in chairs at the dining room table.

"Okay, get him dressed and out of here as fast as possible," ordered the DA.

Just then the paramedics arrived and immediately began to take Officer St. James' vital signs. They called in to the trauma center at Prince George General Hospital to seek advice on the type of immediate treatment needed for St. James.

"Did he actually fuck me?" asked Pat in a much-drugged voice.

"No, Pat. He didn't get that far before I flew through the air and tackled him. But, buddy, you sure came close!" said Hank.

"Sir, we need to know what's going on so that we can advise our headquarters that the governor is no longer under our protection," said one of the troopers.

"Certainly. Let me sit down and I will fill you in on everything up until this point," replied the DA.

As he gave the state police all of the details, the medics had a stretcher brought up. St. James was taken out and rushed to the hospital just to be safe. They could not estimate how much of the suspected tranquilizer was given to Pat, and it was dangerous to his heart. Tests were needed immediately.

WITH St. James gone, the governor under arrest and removed from the hotel, and everything photographed, the tech squad began to dismantle their equipment and remove all of the hidden cameras from the governor's suite.

A press conference was called for 9:00 a.m. the next morning to give the press details of the arrest that had just taken place. All of the evidence was secured and a chain of custody was begun for each tape of the events that night. It was going to be a hectic next day, thought the chief.

Chapter Sixteen
Three Rings of Fun

THE following morning, the press began to assemble at Prince George's County Police Headquarters in Forestville, Maryland. Word had leaked out from hotel employees that something had happened involving the police and the Governor of the State of Maryland. Officer Patrick St. James was being kept in the hospital for observation for at least one day, to make sure he had no negative reaction to the amount of valium that was found in his blood. The police department was advised that the blood levels indicated that St. James could have in no way been able to fight off the governor had he been alone, and in all likelihood would have been the next homicide victim. Dean and Shawn were both at Pat's bedside in a guarded hospital room at Prince George's General Hospital, which had at least two television satellite trucks parked out in front. Hank was at police headquarters along with the district attorney, the police chief, and several lower-ranking police officials. The departmental doctor was also present to handle any medical questions that might arise. The district attorney was in charge of the press conference and had already decided that very limited information was going to be given out to the press that morning.

The Lieutenant Governor and the Maryland Speaker of the House had scheduled a second press conference in Annapolis, which was to follow the press conference in Forestville. State officials would announce that the Lieutenant Governor would become acting Governor of the state while the criminal matter worked its way through the courts, or if the Governor resigned his position. If the latter occurred, the Lieutenant Governor would become the Governor.

The tension was high among the members of the press while they waited for official word on what had happened the night before. All of the national news networks were also present in addition to the local media. The sharks had all smelled blood in the water, and they were circling for the killer headlines.

At the hospital, the television was turned on in Pat's room as they all watched the anticipated news conference.

"Pat, once again you've stuck your neck way out and have ended up in the hospital. Are you going to tell me exactly what happened to you?" Dean asked.

"Just another couple of minutes, Dean, and I can tell you everything, but it has to come from the news conference first before it's public information. Just bear with me a little longer, honey."

"You look really tired, Pat. Are you sure you're going to be all right?" asked Shawn.

"Yes. I've been told that I will be back to normal in twenty-four hours or so, and that my staying here tonight is just a precaution."

Just as the nurse left from taking another blood pressure reading from Pat, the news conference started and the room went silent.

"Ladies and gentlemen, I have a brief statement to make, and then the Prince George's County Police Chief will answer very limited questions. Early this morning, at 12:09 a.m., officers of the Prince George's County Police Department arrested Governor Hanes for assault and battery, indecent assault, felony sexual assault, using a drug in the commission of a felony to render a victim unresponsive, attempted rape, and attempted murder of an undercover police officer.

These charges resulted from an undercover operation that took place at the Prince George's County Hilton Hotel in College Park, in which the Governor was the target. This operation was launched when information surfaced and became known to the police and my office that the governor is alleged to have committed at least two murders of young men in the past two years. Circumstances early this morning indicated that the governor would once again attempt to murder a young man, who happened to be a police officer. The officer is resting comfortably at the county hospital and is under police guard. The governor will be brought before the court later this morning for a bail hearing and formally charged with the aforementioned crimes. All of the evidence, including the allegations of homicide, will be presented to a county grand jury that will decide on further charges if any. A separate news conference is being held shortly in Annapolis regarding the political ramifications of the governor's arrest. At this time, I have nothing further to add to this statement and I will not be taking any questions. Chief Morgan will now answer limited questions."

Pandemonium broke out in the room, and it took a couple of minutes to regain order. Every reporter present was shouting questions to the DA, who stoically ignored them all. He was determined not to make any mistakes, such as making an ill-advised statement, which would aid the defense. The chief came forward.

"I'm Chief Morgan of the Prince George's County Police Department. It was our officers in conjunction with the District Attorney's office that coordinated the undercover sting operation that resulted in the arrest of the governor. I don't intend to give out too many details at this time as formal charges have yet to be technically filed with the court. I will take three questions for now."

"Chief, Andrew Carter here, CNN. Can you tell me if this was in fact a sexual sting that involved the governor and a male officer?"

"Yes."

"Jessica Rogers, ABC. Are you saying that the governor is gay?"

"No, I am not speculating on the sexual orientation of the governor. You would have to ask him."

"Anthony Salick, *Washington Post*. Was the officer injured, and if so, what are the nature of his injuries?"

"The officer was not seriously injured but was drugged and is being held for observation. That's all the questions for now, thank you."

As more questions were thrown at the officials and ignored, the DA and the police turned around and left the room through a rear door. This left the press with nothing to do but run to their satellite trucks and cell phones to report in on what had just occurred.

When questioned by the police after his arrest, the governor refused to cooperate and demanded an attorney. He provided the police with the name and number for his personal attorney, and he was contacted to assist the governor. No further questioning took place after that request.

AT 2:00 p.m. with a national press storm running full rage, the governor was brought before a circuit court judge for bail review. Extra police had to be called in from the evening shift for courthouse crowd control and security. Normally bail reviews were done by close-circuit television from the county jail, which eliminated the need to transport prisoners from the secure county jail into public view. But nothing about this case was going to be ordinary, and the governor made a personal appearance before the court, represented by counsel.

"Your honor, we waive formal reading of the charges since the governor has already been advised by the District Court Commissioner at his initial appearance. We request that the court release my client on personal recognizance since he is the Governor of the State of Maryland, and is a very low risk for flight," requested Max Alexander, the governor's attorney.

"What do the people say in this matter?" asked the judge.

"Your honor, we feel to the contrary that the defendant is a flight risk precisely because he is the Governor of Maryland and has connections throughout the world to aid him in disappearing. The people ask that the governor be remanded to jail under at least one million dollars cash bond, as the charges are serious in nature and because, as a direct result of the defendant's actions, a police officer lies in a hospital room as we speak," responded the DA, who was personally handling all aspects of this case.

"Your honor, I object to the district attorney's reasons for such a ridiculously high bail, as it assumes facts not in evidence since this is only a bail hearing and not a trial."

"While this may be just a bail hearing, counselor, there is probable cause as found by the Commissioner and agreed to by the court that the governor did in fact commit the prescribed crimes for which he is charged. While probable cause is not a finding of guilt or innocence, it is an indicator that the governor could very well be a flight risk and a danger to the community. Therefore bail is set at five hundred thousand dollars cash or property. This hearing is adjourned until the preliminary hearing to be held three weeks from today at nine a.m.," said the judge.

As the judge finished his findings, the DA watched the press once again bolt from the courtroom to announce the decision of the court to the world. Maryland's governor was going to jail until such time as a half-million dollar bail was paid.

"Don't worry, Governor; I will have you out by dinner time. You won't be spending even one night in jail," Hanes' attorney assured him.

"You better get me out of here, and fast!"

As the defendant was led away by the sheriff's department, a press conference was begun in Annapolis. As the governor was processed into jail, the State Senate removed him on a temporary basis from his post, and the Lieutenant Governor was appointed Acting Governor until the resolution of the criminal case against the governor was determined.

It was a swift act taken by the state to ensure continued governorship of the state by a person who was not distracted by what had quickly become a national circus. This story had politics, drugs, gay sex, and possibly murder charges down the road. Nothing could have made a better story for the supermarket tabloids, let alone the national mainstream press. This story had "legs."

By now, the governor knew that his chief of staff had sold him out to the cops, and he was livid. All the governor could think about was how to get even with the man he had thought was his trained poodle.

His son, of course! He would make Bill pay by harming his onetime friend's son as soon as he got out on bail. He grew hard just thinking about what he was going to do to the innocent teenager. And that cop! That cute son of a bitch who set him up at the hotel, he would be dealt with also. He would be a much harder case to deal with since he was a cop, but no one was immune to revenge, this he knew.

As promised, the governor's attorney had posted his bail. Hanes was released at 5:05 p.m. and driven away in a Lincoln with tinted windows. At least a hundred reporters waited outside the county jail to get a picture of the once-mighty governor being released from a jail. This time, however, he did not have a state police detail waiting for him to smooth the way. Since he was not the governor at the moment, he lost his security detail and he had to travel the roadways, as a common person would have to travel. He was still permitted to live at the mansion since his family was there, and his removal was at this point not permanent. However, the governor knew that it was bound to become permanent since the police had everything on videotape.

By the time he reached the mansion in Annapolis, he was despondent and was actually frightened at the reaction he would get from his wife and children. How could he have been so stupid as to let himself get baited into that situation? How could he possibly come up with an explanation that was anything but acknowledgment of guilt? That damn cop! They had actually put a young-looking, handsome undercover officer next to him as a waiter, and he fell for it, hook, line, and sinker. It proved to him that the police had studied some of his behavior as well as the type of young guy he liked. The information had to have come from Bill, that traitorous bastard! No one else could have possessed the information necessary for setting this whole sting up. Well, he could forget ever being a congressman! In fact, he could forget about living!

As the now-suspended governor entered the mansion, one thing became obvious rather quickly. It was dead quiet. None of the usual hum of household activity could be heard, nor did the sound of the happy laughs of his daughter that usually reverberated off of the ornate walls come to his ears. What was going on?

Once he entered the private quarters area of the mansion, the reason became clear. He found a note from his wife, which read:

"To say that I am shocked and utterly disgusted with you would be to put it mildly. I watched both the police press conference as well as the conference at the Capitol, and cannot believe what has been revealed about you. Our marriage has been a sham, political theater, a Kabuki sketch, nothing more. For God's sake, you're a cocksucker and a murderer! All the time we've been sharing a bed, you have been out blowing guys you meet on the road. How dare you! You have embarrassed your daughter, our family, and me. I have no choice but to leave you and sue for divorce. I will fight any attempt by you to win custody of our daughter. Whoever heard of a queer governor? Contact Derek Henderson, my attorney, for anything that you want from me. I don't want to even speak to you!"

The note wasn't even signed, but he knew it was from her by the handwriting. What had he done? He was losing his governorship, his wife and only child, his reputation and security in life. It wasn't fair! Others in higher office than he held had far darker secrets than his. What of them? Where were they? Not one had called to offer comfort or assistance. Yes, he liked to have sex with young men, but others had sex with little girls and yet they hadn't had their lives explode across the world stage. Well, something had to give here; he wasn't going to take all of this lying down. It was time to start making some calls to the right people.

THE following day Officer Patrick St. James was released from the hospital and reported to police headquarters as ordered. After his arrival, the DA called a meeting for all of the principle participants in the sting. Pat was greeted once again like something of a hero; word had spread through the department like wildfire that he had gone undercover and nailed the governor of Maryland.

As the room settled down, the DA opened the meeting.

"Good morning, everyone. Well, Officer St. James is out of the hospital as you all can see and reportedly is in fine condition. I can tell you now, that he had a dangerously high level of valium in his system when his blood was tested at the hospital. We all applaud you for your dedication to duty, St. James, and for putting your life on the line once again."

"Thank you, Mr. Jenkins. I'm glad the operation was a success," Pat said.

"Oh, it was by far more than just a success. It was a slam dunk. I doubt if this case will ever go to trial, as I believe that he will plead out on the charges in exchange for life in prison without the possibility of parole instead of the death sentence. The only problem is deciding on whether or not to allow him to do that. We have at least two dead men that we know of, and that is far more serious than the charges related to this sting. I might also caution you, Pat, that you might want to be on your guard more than usual until he is put away. The governor is a powerful man with a lot of connections, and he may have taken this quite personally. As it is, I have requested the state police to keep Bill under police protection until the case is resolved. I don't want anything happening to our star witness or you."

"Speaking of which, Pat, I'm assigning you to the Detective Bureau to work on routine admin work until this is over. I don't want you exposed any more than necessary for the time being," said the chief.

"But Chief, what will Capstone do without me on the streets?"

Laughter broke out among the cops and Hank just turned red.

"Actually, I'm assigning Officer Capstone to you as a protection detail. Again, I want nothing to happen to you as a result of this case."

"Oh, great, now I have to babysit him. It's bad enough I had to teach him everything he knows about police work. Now this!"

"Teach *me*? Ha! That's rich."

Once again, laughter filled the air as the meeting came to a close with a final statement from the DA.

"Okay, pending trial or disposition of this case, no one talks to the press. My press people will handle all press inquiries in order to maintain control over information that is being dispensed for public consumption. By the way, I have already had a call from the White House on this arrest, and I am expecting a call from the Justice Department as well. We have to be absolutely correct in everything we do in this case, because powerful people will be looking for ways to screw this case up before the courts decide it. Politics is going to be ever-present at every turn we take. Should any of you have any questions about this case, contact me directly."

With that the meeting came to a close. The chief approached Pat.

"Okay, take the rest of the week off on sick leave before you report to the Detective Bureau. It's going to take you a bit of time for that entire drug dose to be out of your system, so just rest for now. Capstone, stick with your partner and make sure nothing happens to him, understand?"

"Sure, Chief. Not a problem at all."

"By the way, Pat, I'm putting you up for a meritorious service award for this investigation. You earned it. Now stay safe, and see you next week."

As Pat and Hank left police headquarters, Hank grabbed Pat's arm to stop him.

"Look, Pat, I would feel a lot better if I stayed real close to you for awhile. I think I should stay at your house while all this is so hot. I think the chief is right; there might be some danger in this for you, and that includes Dean."

"Until you mentioned Dean, there was no way I was going to allow you to babysit me twenty-four/seven, but Dean does change the equation. I would die if anything happened to him because of my job. Okay, you got a deal. Get your shit and come on over this afternoon and I'll let Dean know. But, try not to get Dean any more alarmed than he already is over this whole thing."

"What about Shawn? Can I tell him what's going on?"

"Sure, if you feel you know him well enough now to trust him with this kind of information. That's your call. Hell, you can have him stay at my house too if you want, but he has to be told of the danger that he might be in by being that close to me."

"Deal, partner, I'll see you in an hour or so."

AFTER he got home, Pat made sure the guest room was in top shape for his "bodyguard" and checked the refrigerator to make sure there was enough food in the house for at least a couple of days. He would definitely need to shop, with an extra mouth or two to feed. He decided to call Dean at work and let him know he was home and off for the rest of the week. He also made sure that Dean had no issues with Hank staying at the house for a short time. While Dean was concerned by this news, he did not object and said it might even be fun. Once Dean found out why Hank was staying with them, he might not think it was so much fun.

Chapter Seventeen
"Street Justice"

THE now ex-governor stood in the courtroom next to his high-priced defense team. He had gone overboard and spent tens of thousands on defense attorneys, trying to stay out of jail even though he was impeached and removed from office by the state senate.

He had lost everything because he had come to believe that he was above the law. He had let power corrupt him.

The man in the courtroom was a shadow of the man who had killed his victims in the hotel rooms. He was now standing there as the coward he always was; no more governorship to hide behind, no more protection detail, no more power or money to get him whatever he wanted.

There he stood, just a man in an expensive suit who had committed horrible crimes against young men because he just could not bring himself to admit he was gay.

He was truly pathetic.

As the prosecutor DA Jenkins spoke about the evidence that he would be presenting at trial, Hanes just sat there behind the solid oak table trying to think of ways he could save his ass.

The ex-governor had no remorse for what he had done and, in fact, sometimes late at night, he would masturbate thinking of what he done to those hot young guys. The only thing the governor thought about while he was in the courtroom was how he could parlay this trial into a win for himself.

He knew he was facing the death penalty for his crimes. He knew the evidence against him was overwhelming and that the DA had no interest in his copping a plea. And he understood why he felt that way. The DA had his sights on a higher office in the government, and winning this case was the boost he would need to pursue that goal.

The lawyers concluded the discovery hearing after six hours of testimony. The ex-governor and his lead defense counsel got into a black Lincoln Town Car that was waiting for them outside of the courthouse and left for the mansion.

"Mr. Hanes, after hearing what they are going to present, and seeing their case for what it is, we are going to get clobbered in a trial. I mean, my God, what were you thinking? This is some sick shit," said the lawyer after raising the privacy screen between them and the driver.

"I'm not done yet. I've still got friends who owe me. There's no way I'm going to see a prison or die for this shit," said the governor matter-of-factly.

"What do you mean?" inquired the curious lawyer.

"Let's just say not everyone in the federal government is as pure as they'd like to pretend. I have a call to make on the secure line to the White House when I get home," said the governor.

The lawyer sat back and made notes in the file, paying no further attention to the madman in the seat next to him. Whatever that man had planned, he did not want to know.

The Town Car arrived at its destination. Its occupants found that there were cars in the driveway. The acting governor who had been appointed weeks earlier was starting to use the ex-governor's office as his headquarters to carry out affairs of state.

"Fucking asshole can't even wait until the body's cold. The Democrats are going to be all over this come election time. So much for a Republican majority," mumbled the former governor through his clenched jaw.

"Okay, tomorrow we have suppression motions to go over so I'll be by around nine, Mr. Hanes," said the attorney as the ex-governor closed the car door.

Suppression motions, discovery phase – this was all Greek to the ex-governor. All he could think about was who he was going to call to save his ass when he got into his old office on the secure line.

The secure line was a special phone that didn't have a dial pad; all it had were numerous buttons that went directly into the office of the person the caller wished to speak with. No secretaries, no operators, and no one to intercept the call.

The only people authorized to speak on these lines were the officials themselves.

The ex-governor picked up the shiny black receiver and pushed a series of buttons. There were no names next to the buttons for security reasons. The only thing the caller needed was just a six-digit identification number.

A man answered on the other end and asked for a security code:

"7772 – identify yourself and confirm the line is secure."

The ex-governor replied "0826" and then pushed a button to confirm the line was secure. A light came on a few seconds later and Hanes replied, "Line is confirmed secure."

The man on the other end reconfirmed the security of the line.

"Well, Mr. Hanes, I haven't heard from you in awhile. I've actually missed talking to you," said the voice.

"You're right. It has been too long; your phone dials out too, you know," said the ex-governor.

"Yeah, well, after seeing CNN recently I decided it might be best not to call on you. It seems you're a little busy," said the man on the other end, chuckling.

"Well, you know government is a dirty business. I watch CNN too; you're no stranger to controversy," said Hanes in an annoyed tone.

"Okay, cut the shit. I'm a busy guy. What is it that you want?" asked the government official.

"How about a lifeline, Rick?" asked the ex-governor.

"First of all, you asshole, even on a secure connection you are to never use my name! Second, I have you on tape carrying out your little meetings with these boys, so let's not play any games here," said the man in an angry tone.

"Yes, videotapes can be helpful when shown to juries. I always taped my meetings, all of them." The ex-governor paused and asked, "Why the hell were you taping me?"

"It's part of my job to know what's going on, Mr. Hanes. Your tastes are well-documented; I mean, hell, I've been watching you since the DC boy and that was over two years ago," said the man smugly.

"Oh, so you're going to just let me hang here? After all I've done for you, after the shit we've done together! Well, I guess CNN just got their top story of the year," said the former governor. "If I'm found guilty and I even *see* the inside of a jail cell, I'll be sure to keep the bottom bunk warm for you, because you'll be joining me. I'm going to pass out every photo, recorded cell phone conversation, and office meeting tape to the media. I think they'll love what really happened to that liberal Democratic senator's plane that crashed!" yelled the ex-governor as he slammed down the phone.

Hanes was satisfied that he got his point across. He waited a few seconds, knowing the phone would ring. No one that high up wants to be brought down. The fall would kill him.

Sure enough, the phone rang.

"0826, identify and confirm the line is secure," said Hanes with a smile.

"7772 and confirmed. I can't stop them from finding you guilty and sentencing the 'death with dignity' governor to death. The DA on the case wants to be Attorney General some day, and putting your slimy ass to death might just land him there. However, you won't see the inside of a cell; you will be pulled out before you get to the jail. I'll make the arrangements. You know how this works so just go with his guys when they show up, and you're out," the man on the other end ordered and then hung up.

The ex-governor smiled. He knew he had accomplished his mission so he decided that tomorrow he would just change his plea to guilty and waive all appeals. That would expedite sentencing and the subsequent transport to prison and, finally, his escape.

Hanes had nothing keeping him here any longer: his wife and daughter were gone, his job was gone, his money was gone (except his overseas accounts that were hidden), and his name was destroyed. This was as graceful an exit as he could get and he would take it.

The unidentified man who was helping the ex-governor picked up his phone once more and pressed the bottom button.

Task Force

"0000 – identify yourself and confirm line is secure," said the man.

"7772 confirmed. Meet me in my office in ten minutes. We will have some coffee, and then I have a package for you to deliver at the post office." 7772 hung up and smiled.

THE ex-governor's attorney showed up the next day, promptly pulling into the mansion driveway at 9:00 a.m. He and three other people got out of the black Lincoln Town Car and were let in by the doorman.

"Good Morning Mr. Hanes. I hope you slept well. It's going to be a long one today," said the chief defense counsel.

"Nope. It's going to be really short," said the ex-governor curtly. "Schedule a guilty plea and file for a waiver of all appeals."

"Are you nuts?" asked one of the attorneys. "You'll be executed for sure within five years." There was some mumbling as all of the lawyers looked confusedly at one another.

"Look, I did it, boys. You saw the evidence. I'm fucked," Hanes said, taking on a false sense of remorse. "I feel terrible and the people of the state of Maryland should not have to pay for a lengthy trial and appeals," he said as he sat down in what used to be his study.

The chief defense counsel didn't buy this fake show, so he told the other lawyers to leave the room for a minute.

"Okay, cut the shit; if you have some deal in the works that gets you off, I want in on it," said the chief counsel.

"What are you talking about?" asked the ex-governor, faking confusion as best as he could.

"I know you have friends in high and low places; you told me yourself. So not for one second do I believe you're just going to plead out and let them kill you," the lawyer said, annoyed at the prospect of not getting the press for defending this man and saving his life.

"Look, I'm serious. It's over. If you can't bring yourself to do it, then I'll just hire some fresh-out-of-law-school graduate to do it for me. And much cheaper, I might add," Hanes threatened.

"Take a day or two to think about it. Then I'll do what you want," begged the chief counsel.

"Fine, but my mind's made up," said the ex-governor.

When the attorneys left the mansion, they discussed Hanes' request and wondered when he had lost his mind.

The former governor watched them from the window and smiled to himself, knowing he wouldn't spend a second in a jail regardless of what the twelve morons on the jury said; or, for that matter, that power-hungry DA.

"I'll have to see what I can do to derail that DA's political career. He thinks he can just fuck with me and have no problems. Who does he think he is?" the ex-governor asked himself.

Shawn elected not to sleep at Pat's house with Hank, worried about interfering with the reason Hank was sleeping there in the first place. He preferred to see Hank during the evening, and then return to his own apartment. Dean and Pat quickly adjusted to having Hank around the house, especially since they knew it was only temporary. After what had happened at the campground, they all felt more like family than friends. They talked about the hot night in the tent occasionally, but none of the men knew if anything like it would ever be repeated. Dean's affection for Hank was growing and he was thankful to him for being around and helping to protect Pat.

As for Hank, it didn't hurt that he got to see both Pat and Dean running around naked to the bathroom and other places in the house. They both were a sight to behold, and Hank still remembered the sweet taste of Dean's big cock. Too bad he didn't get the chance to fuck Dean as well.

HANES sat in the defendant's chair. It had been a long month of filing all of the necessary paperwork to waive all of his appeals, as well as officially resigning from the governorship and moving out of the mansion.

As expected, the DA had gone for the death penalty and was at this moment in front of the judge vehemently arguing why the ex-governor should be put to death for his crimes.

"This man drugged, raped, and killed three innocent, promising young men," said Jenkins. "He even tried to rape and kill an undercover police officer! He used his office and power to lure these boys into his arms, knowing they were all vulnerable. All of them were young and impressed by the governor taking an interest in them. The governor even promised the security officer victim a job as a Maryland State Trooper, and when he resisted his sexual advances, this man drugged and raped him. He then strangled him with his own belt. Evidence gathered subsequent to a search warrant found over a half-dozen belts that the defendant had kept as some kind of macabre souvenir from the men he killed. His sick and twisted mind is a danger to society and the only way to protect society is to give him the death penalty. I implore you to impose upon the defendant the ultimate punishment: the death penalty." The ex-governor had tried his best to screw with Mr. Jenkins' career. However, due to his current problems, no one would take his calls. He had become a leper and no one wanted to catch what he had.

The governor had been informed by "7772" that he would be extracted en route to the prison today. He was told to have his seat belt on and just let "7772's" men do their work and he would be a free man.

The judge listened to the defense attorney's impassioned pleas to spare the life of this man, who had served the state of Maryland for so many years; the man who tried to do so much good for so many.

The judge almost rolled his eyes at what the defense counsel was saying. The defense attorney already knew every word he was uttering to defend this maniac was pure bullshit, and he in fact did believe that his client should get gang-raped in prison for the rest of his life as a far more fitting punishment.

The judge called a recess and retreated to his chambers before delivering the sentence. Everyone in the courtroom was sure that the ex-governor was a dead man.

As expected, the judge emerged fifteen minutes later with the sentence of death by lethal injection.

"Bailiffs, take custody of this man and have him transported to the Department of Corrections for execution of sentence," ordered the judge.

The ex-governor showed no emotion upon hearing his sentence, as it was no shock. As governor, Hanes had signed death warrants for less, so he knew it wouldn't be hard for the DA to get his wish.

The bailiffs escorted the ex-governor to the back room, where he was stripped of his suit and given an orange jumpsuit to wear, along with leg irons and a transport belt.

PAT and Hank were present at the sentencing. They weren't sure how they felt about someone they arrested being put to death. Pat knew he wanted to see the man one last time before he was locked away and killed.

Both officers had no trouble gaining access to the prisoner area of the courthouse; they just flashed their badges and were waved in.

They were, however, stopped outside of the room the governor was changing in.

"Sorry, fellas. He's in the custody of the Bureau of Prisons now and it's against policy to let you guys in there. I will let you stay here while he's being walked out to the van and you can have your say then. Just don't do anything stupid, okay?" the older guard said as he winked.

Hank and Pat waited patiently as the ex-governor was prepared. The door finally opened five minutes later and two guards appeared with Hanes in tow.

The former governor looked directly into Pat's eyes, as if to say "I wish I had killed you."

Pat placed his hands behind his back and leaned toward the shackled ex-governor and whispered into his ear, "You're a fucking coward. But don't worry: you'll be getting what you deserve, you son of a bitch."

The ex-governor stopped without breaking his stare and said, "You had over a month to come up with something and that's the best you can do? I should have fucked your ass."

Hanes broke his stare and continued to walk with the guards.

Pat wasn't as satisfied as he had hoped he would be after telling the creature that almost killed him what he thought of him.

Hank put his hand on Pat's shoulder and said, "Let's go, man. It's over. We only have to see him one more time, and that's when he has a needle in his arm."

Hank and Pat walked out of the courthouse and got into their patrol vehicle and left.

THE ex-governor was loaded into the transport vehicle, which was a regular police sedan. There had been a lot of special arrangements made for the transport of the now convicted ex-governor.

The Bureau of Prisons did not want him exposed to the other prisoners because it might have caused a riot, so they assigned these two officers and a sedan to transport him to the maximum-security death row area of the prison in Baltimore.

The two officers buckled the ex-governor in and closed the door. Hanes had heard Hank's comment about the needle in his arm. He had been planning for his future, post-escape, and laughed about the officers thinking they would see him die.

The guards radioed in to their dispatcher that they were secure and moving. The dispatcher advised them that their preplanned route was blocked by a motor vehicle accident with injuries and they were advised to use an alternate route.

The guards looked at each other and one of them said, "That's weird. We never use that route, even when the primary is blocked."

"Yeah, well, this guy's special and all. I guess it's an issue that the brass are dealing with, and as you know, they never consult the guys in the field. What a bunch of shit," said the front passenger.

"What else is new?"

"Dispatch, couldn't we just stick to the highway? It would be quicker," the driver said as he spoke into the microphone.

"Negative. There is too much construction on the highway. Just carry out your orders."

The driver let out a sigh and slammed the microphone down.

"I hate this fucking job," said the passenger.

The ex-governor sat in the back and listened to the exchange between the two guards.

What a couple of idiots. It wouldn't be a shame if they were killed in the escape, Hanes thought to himself as they merged onto the roadway.

It was a nice ride for the most part. The two guards in the front exchanged barbs about how they hated their jobs and the ex-governor sat patiently in the back waiting for the unnamed man to fulfill his promise.

The cell phone of the front seat passenger beeped, alerting its owner that there was no signal.

"I just lost all service on my phone. I hate this cell phone company, and I can't wait until my contract is up."

Then another beep was heard. This time the driver's cell phone lost all service.

"Weird. Mine lost all signal too. I guess it's just the area."

"Hey, why did you change the radio station? I liked that song," said the driver.

"What are you talking about? I didn't touch the radio," said the passenger defensively.

"Man. This is a bad area. No phone, no radio."

The governor knew what was happening and checked his seat belt to make sure it was securely fastened.

"Look at this asshole coming up behind us," said the driver.

"A big expensive SUV like that, and they think they can drive anyway they want," said the passenger.

"Weird. There's two of them. I'm getting a bad feeling here, Larry," said the driver."Radio dispatch and check in." He tried to mask his apprehension.

"It's not working. It's transmitting, but they aren't answering," the passenger said as he swallowed hard.

The two men could feel deep down that something bad was about to happen. They felt it in their heads and in their guts.

Just then the lead SUV sped past the transporting vehicle and cut in front of it, slamming on its brakes.

The former governor watched as the driver of the prisoner transport vehicle tried to avoid rear-ending the big black SUV, but was then struck by the second SUV.

The prisoner transport vehicle spun out into a cement Jersey barrier and the airbags deployed. The two SUVs pinned the prisoner transport vehicle so it could not move. Two men in black ski masks shot through the guards' open windows and hit both correctional officers with some type of tranquilizer dart.

Both of the guards passed out within seconds. The road was deserted except for the two SUVs and the prisoner vehicle.

A man in a black outfit and ski mask unlocked the backdoors using the power locks and grabbed the ex-governor.

The ex-governor was a little dazed himself from the crash, but he was able to stumble to the nearest SUV and get in.

The entire operation was over in less than thirty seconds; the SUVs were out of sight within a minute.

One of the men in the lead SUV waited until they were ten miles away and then dialed 911 for an ambulance for the two guards. They had made sure the dosages in the darts would keep both men out for at least four hours. They were ordered not to kill the guards if at all possible.

The men drove for forty minutes without saying a word as the ex-governor began to recover from what had just happened.

"You guys are good. A little crazy, but damn good," said Hanes as he began to feel a rush of freedom.

"I'm sure one of you has a handcuff key. Can I have it please? These shackles are digging in."

The men did not acknowledge, move, speak, or comply with Hanes' request. It was as if he wasn't even in the vehicle.

The two SUVs pulled into what looked like an abandoned warehousing complex, and the vehicles came to a stop near a helicopter.

"You guys pulled out all the stops for this one, didn't ya?" asked the ex-governor, smiling at the thought of flying to freedom in the chopper.

The front passenger got out of the SUV and opened the ex-governor's door.

"My orders are to retrieve the tapes you spoke of as well as any other media you have," stated the man like a trained drone.

"Oh, you'd like that, wouldn't you? Then you turn me back over to the police. No way! Once I'm on foreign soil you can have all of the stuff," said the ex-governor sternly.

The man only identified as 7772 exited the chopper and walked over to the orange-clad man in shackles.

"You know how this works. I've never burned you on a deal before and we've been in on things much bigger than this. I could never turn you over to the police. I'd just be giving you more leverage if I did that now. So come on. Where's the stuff?" he asked as he put his arm around Hanes.

"There's a package I keep in…." the ex-governor started but was stopped by one of the men clad in black who was pulling something from the back of one of the SUVs.

"A package in your ex-wife's safety deposit box?" the man clad in black said, holding a package the ex-governor was all too familiar with.

"You see, the problem here, Mr. Hanes, is I don't trust you and you're just not any good at this game. I told you we've been watching every move you made ever since we found out you had a weakness for boys," said the man in an expensive suit.

"You being a faggot don't even bother me. What bothers me is you tried to play games and I'm not one of your little boy toys to drug and rape," he continued. "You're a cancer and my job is to cut out any cancers that could harm this administration."

"I was going to give it to you, honest to God," the ex-governor said as tears began welling up in his eyes.

One of the men clad in black picked up a hoist chain from the ground and placed it in the loop on the transport belt. With the click of a button, the orange-clad prisoner was hanging from his waist.

The man known as "7772" looked at the man holding the package and nodded to him. The package was given to 7772, who then gave the final order.

"Make sure he's never found. You see, Governor, I told you that you would never make it to a jail cell, and I keep my word," said the man as he closed the helicopter door and took off.

The men clad in black pulled out a red tool kit and opened it. It contained razor blades, hammers, and bottles of acid.

They expertly voided the orange-clad prisoner of any identifying characteristics; this wasn't their first rodeo and they knew what they were doing.

It was a grisly scene, and in the end even the ex-governor's dog wouldn't have been able to identify what was left of this sociopath. The men loaded the pieces into a wood chipper, making chum of the ex-governor, and then threw his remains in a bag. A cleanup team would pick up the bag, and it would be disposed of off the Atlantic seaboard of the United States.

All of the men stripped and burned their clothing. They then changed into suits, put on sunglasses, and quickly drove away in their government-issued SUVs.

The next day it was all over the news. The headlines read: "Ex-governor escapes after car crash during transport to death row."

PAT finished reading the story and decided to call Hank at home.

"Hank, can you believe this? That psycho is roaming around free with revenge on his mind. Do you think he'll come for us?" he asked.

"God, I hope not. That guy is one sick fuck. Dean is going to be worried sick over this, and so is Shawn," said Hank.

"Look at this. It says the FBI arrived on-scene within fifteen minutes and took control of the crash scene, pulling rank because of who was in the crash and his connections," said Pat, thinking that it was very odd that the FBI would take a crash away from a local police department.

"You don't think his connections bailed him out, do you?" asked Hank.

"I don't know. The whole thing is screwy," Pat replied.

"Well, I'm off to the gym. Time to scope out the hotties while I work on my biceps," Hank said just before he said goodbye and hung up.

PAT and Hank arrived at work that night, a little concerned that something might happen to them because of the ex-governor's escape. They both wondered if he would get his final revenge.

"Hey, guys. How's life going?" asked Sergeant Durkin.

"Not bad. Little shook up that the slime ball escaped and is at large," Pat said.

"Well, the FBI took the case from the state and they said the case is closed. Someone killed Hanes and his body was located. However, they won't let us see the body or give us a copy of the file."

"Damn! Well, someone just saved the state a lot of money," Pat said with a smile.

"Fucking Feds," said Durkin. "Okay, everyone. Roll call!"

John Simpson, a Vietnam era Veteran, has been a uniformed Police Officer of the year, a Federal Agent, a Federal Magistrate, an armed bodyguard to royalty and a senior Government executive, with awards from the Vice-President of the United States and the Secretary of the Treasury. John now writes and is the author of *Murder Most Gay*, a full-length novel, with a sequel entitled *Task Force*, both published through Dreamspinner Press, and numerous short stories for Alyson Books. Additionally, he has written articles for various gay and straight magazines. John lives with his partner of 35 years and three wonderful Scott Terriers, all spoiled. John is also involved with the Old Catholic Church and its liberal pastoral positions on the Gay community.

Visit John's Website at www.johnsimpsonbooks.com

Novels from Dreamspinner Press

Alliance in Blood by Ariel Tachna 232 pages
Paperback $11.99 eBook $5.99
ISBN: 978-0-9815084-9-8 ISBN: 978-0-9817372-1-8

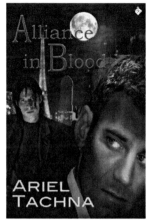

Can a desperate wizard and a bitter, disillusioned vampire find a way to build the partnership that could save their world?

In a world rocked by magical war, vampires are seen by many as less than human, as the stereotypical creatures of the night who prey on others. But as the war intensifies, the wizards know they need an advantage to turn the tide in their favor: the strength and edge the vampires can give them in the battle against the dark wizards who seek to destroy life as they know it.

In a dangerous move and show of good will, the wizards ask the leader of the vampires to meet with them, so that they might plead their cause. One desperate man, Alain Magnier, and one bitter, disillusioned vampire, Orlando St. Clair, meet in Paris, and the fate of the world hangs in the balance of their decision: Will the vampires join the cause and form a partnership with the wizards to win the war?

The first of a four part series.

The Archer by Abigail Roux 576 pages
Paperback $19.99 eBook $8.99
ISBN: 978-0-9815084-8-1 ISBN: 978-0-9817372-0-1

Rocked to the core by traitors and spies, the Organization made an unprecedented move in bringing together six highly trained men to track down one rogue wolf: The Archer.

There are three field agents: one at the top of his game, one hoping to retire, and another walking the line; a cold-blooded assassin who can use any weapon known to man; a demolitions expert who can't resist the allure of fire; and a computer hacker with more tricks in his mouse than Houdini. This team is made up of the best of the best, and if it can't succeed in this impossible mission, no one can. But no plan survives first contact with the enemy – especially when you can't even find out who he is!

Despite what a cluster the assignment is from the start, the six men try to get their act together to track down the rogue operative, and in the process they discover there's more to life than the next assignment. Now it's up to them to survive by working together and determining who the real traitor is: an unknown friend, a close-by enemy, or the Organization itself.

Caught Running by Urban & Roux 236 pages
Paperback $11.99 **eBook** $5.99
ISBN: 978-0-9801018-8-1 ISBN: 978-0-9801018-9-8

Ten years after graduation, Jake "the jock" Campbell and Brandon "the nerd" Bartlett are teaching at their old high school and still living in separate worlds. When Brandon is thrown into a coaching job on Jake's baseball team, they find themselves learning more about each other than they'd ever expected. High school is all about image – even for the teachers. Brandon and Jake have to get past their preconceived notions to find the friendship needed to work together. And somewhere along the way, they discover that perceptions can always change for the better.

Condor One by John Simpson 208 pages
Paperback $11.99 **eBook** $5.99
ISBN: 978-0-9817372-8-7 ISBN: 978-0-9817372-9-4

The Democratic Party's 2012 nominee for President, David J. Windsor, and America are equally shocked when he is outed by his opponent just six weeks before the Fall election. Following his heart, David chooses honesty over media spin and overcomes the obstacle to win the election.

Despite that success, dark forces around the world begin to plot against him, and President Windsor's security is a must. Inside and outside the White House, Secret Service Agent Shane Thompson becomes the President's shadow, always present and silent, ever vigilant.

As the two men grow closer, Shane does far more than just his duty – he becomes as vital to David's happiness as he is to the President's health. Together they realize they must find a way to balance the President and the Agent against David and Shane before stress and responsibility tear them apart.

Cursed by Rhianne Aile
Paperback $11.99
ISBN: 978-0-9795048-2-2

232 pages
eBook $5.99
ISBN: 978-0-9795048-3-9

Upon their grandmother's death, Tristan Northland and his twin, Will, come into possession of her Book of Shadows and the knowledge that their family is responsible for a centuries old curse. Determined to right the ancient wrong, Tristan sets off across the ocean to reverse the dark magic that affects the Sterling family to this day.

Benjamin Sterling might not be happy with his life, but it is predictable – at least until Tristan Northland shows up in his office, unannounced and with nowhere to stay. He has plenty of reason to distrust witches and Northlands, but instead of caution, he experiences two unexpected emotions: hope and love

Diplomacy by Zahra Owens
Paperback $11.99
ISBN: 978-0-9801018-6-7

228 pages
eBook $5.99
ISBN: 978-0-9801018-9-8

Jack Christensen has everything he ever wanted. He's a rising star in US Diplomacy, the youngest man to have been appointed as an Ambassador of the United States. A career diplomat who's just been sent to a politically interesting Embassy in Europe, he has the perfect wife, speaks five languages and has all the right credentials, yet there's something missing and he doesn't quite know what.

Then Lucas Carlton walks into an Embassy reception and introduces himself and his American fiancée. From the first handshake, the young Englishman makes an impression on Jack that leaves him confused and uncharacteristically insecure. Lucas' position as the British liaison to the American Embassy means they are forced to work together closely and they have a hard time denying the attraction between them, despite their current relationships.

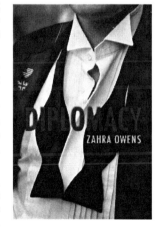

Diplomatic circles are notoriously conservative though, and they each know that the right woman by their side makes a very significant contribution to their success. Will they be able to make the right choices in their professional and personal lives? Or will they need to sacrifice one for the other?

Gold Warrior by Clare London   240 pages
Paperback $11.99   **eBook** $5.99
ISBN: 978-0-9815084-4-3   ISBN: 978-0-9815084-5-0

Maen is a Gold Warrior, a defender of Aza City, a world controlled by the Queen and her womankind where the best of men are maintained for the military and the women's pleasure. A favorite of his imperious Mistress and a leader among his men, Maen is too cautious to seek casual sexual satisfaction and so stays alone, taking his comfort in ensuring a stable and controlled world. That world is thrown into disarray by Dax, a bold and challenging new Bronze soldier who excites Maen with his fierce hero worship and leads them to a forbidden affair. They find themselves thrown together in a dangerous and hostile environment without the support of the City and far away from their loyalties, and Maen finds himself risking everything for Dax – his position; his loyalties; and eventually, his life.

Love Ahead by Urban & Roux   308 pages
Paperback $14.99   **eBook** $6.99
ISBN: 978-0-9817372-4-9   ISBN: 978-0-9817372-5-6

A pair of working man novellas.

Under Contract
Site foreman Ted Lucas moved to Birmingham, leaving a full life behind, only to discover something - someone - to look forward to. Assistant Nick Cooper catches his eye, and even more incredibly, Lucas's heart, all without a word. When Lucas finds out Cooper's asked to be transferred, he bites the bullet and admits his feelings. Intrigued, Cooper offers Lucas one night to figure out if that love could possibly be real.

Over the Road
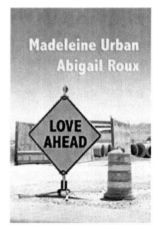

Truck driver Elliot Cochran meets 'McLean' while talking on the CB and strikes up an unusual friendship. One evening, McLean tells Elliot he needs to go find some companionship, and so Elliot meets Jimmy Vaughan - and has one of the best nights in his life. Before long Elliot faces a decision about sharing his life: Does he choose McLean, the best friend he's never met, or Jimmy, the man who thrills him beyond belief.

Murder Most Gay by John Simpson   220 pages
Paperback $11.99   **eBook** $5.99
ISBN: 978-0-9817372-2-5   **ISBN**: 978-0-9817372-3-2

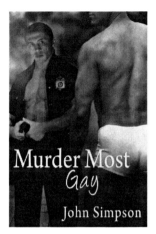

A serial killer is targeting gay men, preying on them in popular bars and parks. Assigned to the case, rookie cop Pat St. James feels all too close to the victims. He's gay and firmly in the closet at work. The fact that he's sent undercover as a gay man is a stroke of irony.

Pat and his fellow cop, Hank, are hanging out in bars, trying to get a lead on the killer. At the same time, Pat's looking for Mr. Right – juggling three men, hoping he'll find the perfect match for himself. He picked up Bill at a bar, Dean's a longtime friend … and in yet another ironic twist, his partner, Hank, is also gay and on the list of possible beaus.

As the killer continues to rampage, strangling and raping his victims, Pat has to focus on his work and hope that his personal life survives the stress. But when his hopes and dreams for happiness overlap with the investigation, Pat may be headed for big trouble.

A Summer Place by Ariel Tachna   248 pages
Paperback $11.99   **eBook** $5.99
ISBN: 978-0-9795048-4-6   **ISBN**: 978-0-9795048-5-3

Overseer Nicolas Wells had been coming to Mount Desert Island for ten summers to help build cottages for the rich and powerful. Despite his secrets, he had grown comfortable in the peaceful little island town, getting to know its inhabitants and even to consider some of them friends. The eleventh year, however, he arrived to startling news: the island's peace had been shattered by a murder. At the request of the sheriff, Shawn Parnell, Nicolas agreed to hire Philip Hall, the local blacksmith and the probable next victim, in the hope that the secure construction site would be safer than his house in the village. He never expected the decision to lead to danger. Or to love.

To Love a Cowboy by Rhianne Aile 228 pages
Paperback $11.99 eBook $5.99
ISBN: 978-0-9795048-8-4 ISBN: 978-0-9795048-9-1

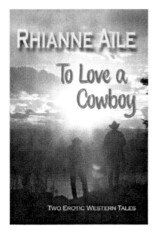

Seven years ago, Roan Bucklin left the family ranch for college, leaving foreman Patrick Lassiter with a mix of sweltering emotions: relief, regret, and nearly overwhelming desire. Afraid that Roan would regret giving himself to an older man, Patrick let him go without a word about his true feelings. But Roan took Patrick's heart with him.

Roan had harbored a crush on Patrick from the time he'd turned fourteen. He thought he'd gotten over it, grown up, moved on, but now he's back and home to stay. After one look, he knows he has something to prove to Patrick – that he wants to be claimed by the cowboy who has always possessed his heart.

Twisted Brand by Clare London 288 pages
Paperback $14.99 eBook $6.99
ISBN: 978-0-9817372-6-3 ISBN: 978-0-9817372-7-0

*Sequel to **The Gold Warrior***

No longer a revered Gold Warrior, Maen is a disgraced soldier, held in suspicion despite his role in winning the Queenship of Aza City for his Mistress, Seleste. Returned alive from his captivity by the rebel Exiles, his reward was to be cast out from his position, his brave loyalty dismissed. He remains an unwilling thrall to the new Queen while his heart mourns the memory of Dax, the young Bronzeman he helped escape from a sentence of death.

When Maen is put under the guard of the arrogant Gold Warrior Zander and given the thankless task of preparing a Royal History, they both join up with the lively scribe Kiel. The youngster's bold curiosity initiates a chain of events that will change their world and that of the City forever. Maen's own discoveries will cast a new and shocking light on the Royal history and stir revolution in both citizens and rebels. And he will finally return to the Exile camp to face the one thing that can make him choose desire over duty.

Printed in the United States
125509LV00003B/1-36/P